Printed in the United States of America

First Printing, 2013

ISBN: 0615816282
ISBN-13: 978-0615816289

 RANTHIA PRESS
Easton, MD

www.TheCageandTheKey.com

The Cage
and
The Key

A Spiritual Sojourn

AMY ABRAMS

ALSO BY AMY ABRAMS

Schenck in the 21st Century: The Myth of the Hero and The Truth of America

Prologue

She nods to the council. An understanding is acknowledged by all that she has agreed. She will undertake the assignment without knowledge of her skills, without access to her power. Placing her palms together in prayer above her head, her silhouette a mountain crest against the full moon, she descends down, liquid silver, magic elixir, changing shape.

Amidst a dream, her identity is erased, yet even upon awakening, she will not remember. To gain awareness of this sacred covenant, she will wait fifty years. Moreover, during this half-century, the pact entails that everything she will come to possess will be lost. This is the key to recovering her self. She alights on Earth, inhabiting the bodily form of Celia Ann Barrens, to grasp this greatest of paradoxes.

Part One

Chapter One

CYNTHIA

IT IS A COMMONLY KNOWN FACT, but not formally documented, that throughout the whole of history, women spend money on frivolity in inverse proportion to the amount of attention and affection they receive from their benefactors, be they husbands or lovers. Cynthia buys clothes and shoes on Friday, as if acquiring attire for an entire chorus line.

That evening, when Benjamin rolls off her and into a sound snore, she silently slides out of bed and showers. The vanity mirror wet with steam, she wipes it clean with a stroke of her hand. Cynthia assesses her face— pouting lips in the shape of a kiss, deep-set steel eyes framed by straight blond hair grazing her slender shoulders, often flipped at the ends for the 1950s trend. Her admirers, of whom there have been many, reference Grace Kelly when describing her demure allure. Beyond the large master bath, the house holds many mirrors, large and small, by which she likes to linger when no one is looking, or casually catch her reflection when passing by. This makes her feel real and alive.

. . .

"Yup, likely two months along," says Dr. Wasserstein with a smile, intending welcome news. *No*, Cynthia thinks, *not another baby, just when my figure's back*. Vivian has just turned 14 months and Cynthia finally squeezes into her favorite size six Chanel skirt.

"I'm just lucky, lucky, lucky," Cynthia says, feigning a smile.

Oblivious to her sarcasm, the doctor beams, "Won't Mr. Barrens be beside himself with joy?"

Cynthia never understood this expression and pictures two of her husband. *Spare me*. Yet, it oddly makes sense. There is the public Benjamin Barrens, the most successful businessman in town, readily greeting neighbors, shopkeepers, and business associates with a hard handshake, a senator's smile. There's the hidden Ben, slowly and with a certain satisfaction, nursing his anger, TV blaring, glued to the game, or ruling the roost sequestered behind *The Baltimore Sun* at the breakfast table, Cynthia tiptoeing around his rousing rage, never knowing what inconspicuous comment or shift in air current might provoke him.

By June, Cynthia has gained 38 pounds. It doesn't help that both Barb and Colette say losing the weight is harder with the second one. Her curvaceous hips make perfect ledges for an infant to sit on, but Cynthia isn't inclined to hold Vivian. If she does pick up her daughter, she dangles her at arm's length to scrutinize her bone structure and hand her, legs flailing, to "the help." That's what Maggie's for.

Chapter Two

CELIA

ONE WEEK FROM HER DUE DATE, Cynthia broods that her days are unjustly reduced to three main activities: sitting on the couch, hoisting herself up, and peeing. When she tries to eat, the baby kicks her in the gut; when she tries to sleep, the baby squarely sits on her bladder. Without so much as laying eyes on this twit, she holds a grudge. Wearing a stretch-waistband black skirt, a white taffeta blouse with a bow at her neck, white stockings and black pumps—and her graceful arms remarkably unaltered by a hefty weight gain—she looks a bit like Humpty Dumpty, as she impatiently awaits Barb and their hair and nails appointment (every Thursday at two).

After a "wash and set," Cynthia and Barb are parked beneath beehive hair dryers with foldable trays placed before them, where a light lunch is served. Barb takes a ladylike bite from her fruit plate. Chicken salad sits on a bed of iceberg lettuce alongside a cellophane packet of Melba Toast for Cynthia. One might surmise that the heat to Cynthia's head, a kind of hard-boiling of the brain, compromises her judgment, or presume that she mistakenly assigns the intermittent pain in her abdomen to a few sharp kicks from the fetus, but truth be told, she stubbornly ignores the tell-tale signs of labor. She recalls Vivian's birth (a godforsaken four hours before Dr. Wasserstein administered the drugs), so she rationalizes...*I have time*. She thinks of Ben and their friends coming to see her and the new arrival, concluding that her hair must be dried, rollers removed, teased, and sprayed. *That's final.* Yet, when the dryer timer goes braaang—forty minutes later—and she's ushered by Bobby, her hairdresser, into his styling station, her contractions are nearing four minutes apart.

The hospital's just 15 minutes up Salisbury Street, she tells herself, the pain mounting, while Bobby pulls out her rollers and picks at her curls with the pointed handle of the comb.

"You OK, Mrs. Barrens?" he asks, noticing a high flush and faint grimace across that awfully pretty face. But before Cynthia can reply, a torrent of amniotic fluid streams down her legs, puddling on the pink linoleum floor. Bobby jumps back and lets loose a high-pitched holler, whipping Barb's head up from her *Ladies Home Journal*—a shrill she hears loud and clear, even above the drone of the two-foot tall contraption encasing her head. Cynthia looks down at her shoes, brand new and ruined...*completely ruined.*

"Cyndi, honey, your water broke!" yells Barb, cranking up her helmet, jumping from her chair, her fruit plate crashing, splaying canned pineapple and maraschino cherries across the floor. "Bobby, call Ben. Call Ben! Tell him meet us at St. Joe's. Cyndi, what's his number?" Doubled over in her chair, Cynthia mumbles the digits. Barb grips Cynthia's elbows, helping her to stand, while shouting directives to the new receptionist, who looks not a day older than 14 and scared: "Grab our pocketbooks—help me to the car!" The other customers, now up from their seats, huddle into groups, one hesitantly offering assistance, relieved to be ignored.

Within a halo of curlers, Barb's brow breaks into a sweat, as she bears the weight of her friend, who sloshes and waddles to the door. With the help of the new girl, not altogether inept, Barb lowers the moaning Cynthia into the passenger seat. As they pull from the parking lot, Bobby dashes outside, comb still in hand, jumps up and down at the curb, as if he's just won something and yells, "We reached Ben—he's on his way!"

The contractions are one on top of another now. Cynthia can hardly catch her breath before another wave hits. She's sure she'll pass out from the pain and she wants more than anything to push—push, push—with all her strength, but she holds tight, not knowing what to do if the baby might, heaven forbid, plop into her pantyhose. She is cold and hot, shivering and sweating, breathing hard like a marathon runner nearing the finish, and then holding her breath, not breathing at all.

"Just hold on. We're almost there, Cyndi darling," Barb consoles, although she's attempting to convince herself, as she floors it. She manages five miles doing 70 in a 40 zone, swerving around the slower moving cars, before she hears the siren and sees the black-and-white police car behind her, lights flashing.

"Lord, no," mutters Barb as she pulls the car to the curb, jumps out, arms flailing, curlers bouncing, screaming back to the officer as he exits his car. "We're having a baby! Like right now!" The officer runs forward and peers inside to find Cynthia curled into a fetus herself, sweating, red-faced and moaning.

"Hospital, hospital," she moans. Cynthia Barrens, finally, is scared.

"Follow me," he announces, securing his cap, taking sleek strides in his shining black boots back to his vehicle, hitting the siren, sounding the wailing. With Barb trailing right behind, they whiz through red lights and stop signs, and screech to a halt at the EMERGENCY ROOM sign in all its red-and-white glory.

While what happens next unfurls in fast-forward—the glass double doors swinging wide, the stretcher surrounded by uniformed orderlies racing to the car, cutting Cynthia's soaked pantyhose and skirt with a surgical scissors, and the baby's head emerging with just three long-awaited pushes—these harried events happen in slow-motion for Cynthia, a morphing of time into a measured sequence of ultra-sensory moments, in which all life-or-death crisis take place. Everything extraneous moves aside, so her body can fully focus on survival and the instinctual furthering of the human race. Her ruined shoes and skirt; her mashed and matted hair; her running mascara play no part. For these few minutes, she is released from herself into the power of the moment, in which earthly life begins for Celia Ann Barrens.

Yet, there is no rejoicing, as is expected of new beginnings, of birth—not on Earth and not high above, beyond the heavens. Curled upon a cumulonimbus cloud, the despairing cry of Lady Kamara echoes around the universe. She begs Lord Myran to retract their daughter's embodiment agreement on Earth. To console his wife, he gently rocks her in his arms and kisses her forehead. From his fingertips sprout fragrant jasmine and jonquils, which he weaves through her waist-length hair. He lassoes light for a necklace of stars, which he laces around her neck.

"You cannot tame her," he offers. "She is stubborn, but her free will cannot be denied. You must come to terms with her rebellious spirit."

Ben Barrens sits impatiently at a red light, when six-pound Celia is hoisted and dangled upside-down by her ankles. With a cry, she gasps her first breath. Summoned by his secretary from the wood-paneled conference room, where he was meeting with Hal Crane, a potential client, Ben felt more aggravated losing the momentum of a sale than excited about a new addition to his family. While he won't admit as much, he hopes for a boy, a son, feeling outnumbered now around the house, three to one, counting the help. He imagines a miniature companion…someone to take to the game, usher into the business, commiserate with about the insanity of women. They'd end each work day with a stiff scotch and cigarette, feet perched on their cherry wood desks, sharing steep profits and private jokes. Bestowed on this imagined son would be all the love and money he never had as a child, a do-over if fate would grant it, to raise a Barrens boy right, God damn it. He lights a cigarette, pulls out the plastic ashtray from the dashboard and blows smoke rings, one inside the other, until they merge and dissipate into the nothingness from which they came.

It's not yet 3:30. Leaving work early on a Friday surprises him with a palpable sense of adventure. *Why veer off at the hospital exit when the highway signs announce directives to the shore?* Fully anonymous, he'd slip into a dimly lit

6

bar, released from every obligation, outstanding balance and chore. He'd take up serious drinking, sleep into the sun-drenched afternoons, wasted from heated romps with women who want him, really want him.

After turning into the freshly paved hospital parking lot, he feels a stab of insult when he can't find a spot up front, close to the entrance, for he possesses a sense of entitlement, encouraged by the frequent acknowledgment of his financial success by the townspeople and town's leaders, who heartily pat him on the back with reference to his "know-how" or "keen insight," or all that he's subsidized (however inadvertently), through tax revenues and employment opportunities in their town of pride. Ben has become increasingly reliant on these soothing infusions to his self-worth. He imagines a sign with his name on it, just like the doctors have earned, his own little plot of privilege. *Reserved: Benjamin Barrens, President, Atlas Tire.*

The double doors whoosh as they part. Ben enters the reverent and orderly St. Joe's. He's reminded of a church or library. White-coated doctors with serious faces hurry down an adjoining hall. Family and friends of loved ones sit fearful, but stoic, in the emergency room's designated, disinfected waiting area, reading old newspapers, sipping cold coffee, awaiting news. He prides himself on a stirring of sympathy for the fellow members of his community, who suffer in silence, enduring life's haphazard blows.

As Ben approaches the triage desk, he feels apprehension. *Complications*, he imagines Wasserstein saying. That's the dreaded word. *Nowadays, stuff like that doesn't happen in childbirth*, he consoles himself, as a fleeting memory of Cynthia surfaces, when he first saw her at the shore, her slender brown legs against her pale blue bathing suit, her white-blond hair waving in the ocean breeze like a flag of surrender. Merely by comparison, her frailty gave him strength. He believed then, that his manhood would protect her from the countless threats and harms of the world and, in return, her beauty would save him.

"I'm Ben Barrens. My wife, Cynthia, is having a baby." These sparse words, uttered to the young man at the desk, make it so, and now, with a sudden sense of urgency, he wants to know where she is, what the hell is happening.

Chapter Three

MAGGIE

"THE WHOLE HOUSE STINKS LIKE A BABY," Ben grumbles when he arrives home after playing 18 holes, grabbing a beer, slamming shut the icebox door, so all the condiments shake and rattle. His daughters sit side-by-side at the kitchen table: Celia in her high chair, drooling on her Dumbo terry bib—nearing her first birthday, Vivian in yellow-bowed pigtails, squirming in her seat—almost three. Maggie has laid out Cheerios and sliced American cheese on pink plastic plates. The girls are freshly bathed and Mr. Barrens must have been smelling that baby powder, that baby lotion. Maggie knows to keep her mouth shut, her eyes set on those suds she sloshes around in the sink. She gets that feeling right in her gut to ball up and shrink out of sight like an animal attempting camouflage. This trick she learned early on, when her daddy went looking for someplace to hang his humiliation, like that time he twisted her arm so far behind her back, her shoulder dislocated. When Fat Aunt Jean popped it back into place, Maggie fainted.

"Lord have mercy," Maggie mutters beneath her breath, as she wipes dry the flecked Formica counter, while Mr. Barrens finally makes his way to the den with an extra beer. Maggie is in almost constant conversation with the Lord, for He (a white man, no less), looked down from his gold-gated heaven and plucked her out of poverty and shame to secure work that suits her just fine, a housemaid, all because she prayed for salvation (and just occasionally, mind you), her dimpled bare knees pressed hard against the dusty wood floor boards of her bedroom, the room she shared with two older sisters. These three daughters of a whiskey-breathed, perpetually sty-eyed odd-jobber and his bone-tired wife, a washwoman for 17 years, fought for life's bare necessities: grease-fried potatoes for supper dug up from their plot's hard soil and shoes to trek the three-and-a-half miles to school.

Cynthia, or Mrs. Barrens, as Maggie is advised to call her, like many well-off suburban Maryland women of her day, found black housemaids by driving south—with their husbands behind the wheel—into Maryland's and Virginia's farmlands, down dusty roads, pulling their finned Oldsmobiles or Cadillacs up to the shacks that some folks call home. Here, young girls, if they inhabited the house, would line up at the car for inspection and potential selection. If a young, strong contender was fortunate enough to be chosen, she might go back inside to grab whatever's rightly hers, before sliding along the backseat to head to her new home, where she'd receive room and board, as well as wages.

Maggie places two torn dresses, undergarments, a nub of a pencil and a picture postcard of an azure-robed Jesus—his heart beaming a hit-the-jackpot light, into a faded and frayed bandana and knots it tight. She thinks about taking her metal milk pail that swings on her arm on her way to school each morning, to knock the Jaris brothers right up the side of their fat heads if they gave her trouble, but she reckons she ain't got no use for that bucket no more. Amen. She'll miss just one thing: her sweet mama, the love in her life, who stands at the door, crying tears of happiness and sadness all at once, for a better future for her daughter, for a future that won't include her.

He just ain't the same man, Maggie thinks, recollectin' how Mr. Barrens paraded Vivian in that new white carriage up and down the block, sometimes 'round the whole neighborhood, his chest high, beaming that pride of a new papa, just like the crowing red rooster on Hadley's farm.

And it was Mr. Barrens who wanted those family portraits taken, which Maggie tucked into holiday cards and Mrs. Barrens addressed in fancy writing.

Cynthia is also imagining earlier times…when Matterick Van Lines signed and then, Ben got the regional contract for both car and truck tires from Amity National. That spring, they sold the ranch on Sedgewick and moved to Grant Avenue. For Mother's Day, Ben came home with a white mink stole and a double string of pearls, telling her she looked sexy, all full and round like that, carrying his child. Maggie was hired when the baby was born, moved into the maid's room off the kitchen, and by July they had a new set of friends at Bonnieville Country Club. Cynthia seamlessly slipped into her new status with a taste for fitted wool suits and tortoise shell sunglasses, pastel silk scarves tied atop her French bun (for Sunday drives when they lowered the top of the convertible), and brown leather pumps with low wood heels. Barb—whose family legacy was textiles—quipped with earnest affection, "Cyndi darlin', you do 'old money' better than any 'new money' woman I know."

. . .

"You did, too, and you know it," Cynthia frowns at Ben, pushing her chair back, crossing her arms. They're seated at a round, linen-clothed dining table at the club. It's Saturday night, when they dine with Barb and Nick, and Colette and Gerald. Empty gin and martini glasses; cracked lobster claws and lemon rinds; the left-over fatty edges of roast beef, and untouched bowls of creamed spinach are whisked away by black-coated waiters, while orders for tea and coffee and "maybe just a sliver of something sweet," are placed.

"Ben, you remember. You made me try on the mink and pearls with nothing else on and you know it," Cynthia continues. After a few too many gin and tonics, it was Gerald who released Cynthia's "nude modeling" secret at the dinner table, after his wife, Colette, shared Cynthia's admission with him. With a red-lipsticked pout, Cynthia feigns irritation at Colette's betrayal, but clandestinely adores the attention. Colette is furious with her husband's crassness, but saves her condemnations for their ride home that night.

"I'll give you a peep show, too, if you buy me furs and jewels," says Barb, leaning over and pecking her husband Nick on the cheek, then beaming him a wide smile. All eyes are on Nick for a witty reply, but he's slow on a comeback, picturing Cynthia's bare breasts beneath mink.

"She wants me to pay for a peep show," he pipes up, addressing Ben and Gerald. "I was doing that before we got married." This sends the men into laughter and the women dart smirks across the table, but enjoy the jokes.

Ben watches Barb give a soft punch to Nick's arm, longing for the playfulness between them. He feels a sudden stirring beneath his starched white linen napkin, an unexpected longing for Barb...her large, square, capable shoulders, that straightforward Midwestern know-how she has. If he cracked Cynthia's cast, he wonders, would he find something real there, like that.

Ben and Cynthia drive home in silence. At half-past midnight, the Dutch Colonials lining Grant Avenue are dark save foyer lights that burn lonely all night. Only a few homes cast a dim blue TV light in downstairs dens or upstairs bedrooms. The houses get larger as they proceed north along the oak tree-lined avenue, their pale blue Cadillac cruising silently like a big boat. Their cul-de-sac is the most prestigious—the floor plans comprised of five bedrooms on full-acre lots, white brick fireplaces, sunken living rooms with shag carpets, slate patios for outdoor dining, and adjacent grassy areas for swing sets and sandboxes. The precise orderliness placates Cynthia's fears of residing in a man's world. Ben is confined by this rigidity, as if someone or something is holding him back. He intuits the presence of smaller towns to the south, where crime is frequent, where dusty lots are vacant, where the aggressions of men are vivid and fragrant. He senses his own dark past crouched and lurking on the edge of his tidy landscaped lawn, threatening to stagger out, to attack.

. . .

The signs are subtle, at first. Ben no longer takes drives with Cynthia and the two girls on Sunday mornings. He loses weight...his suit jackets buckle at his shoulders, hang loose through the back. His gait changes. It is slower, as if each step requires effort, a succession of deliberate intents to keep moving…keep moving forward. Sometimes, all activity ceases. Cynthia watches him from the kitchen window sitting on the deck, looking out into space. *Is losing the Hertzfeld contract sending him into a tailspin?* Cynthia can't figure it out.

In bed, he doesn't roll on top of her. At first, this is an answered prayer. No longer does she dread turning off the bedside lamp, untying her silk robe, sliding between the sheets. But she worries there's another woman, evaluating the potential threats…*Linda or Ellen in the front office? Impossible. What about Jack Kincaid's sister who recently moved down from New York? She's pretty—and loose. "Those New York divorcees have a reputation," Colette warned. But no, fortunately, none of that feels possible.*

A doctor's appointment is set, yet the checkup and bloodwork reveal nothing out of the ordinary. "Everyone wants numbers like these, Mr. Barrens. You're a fine specimen of health. A little 'R and R' is in order. Relax a bit. Less stress, hmm?"

Ben readily falls asleep at night, but often wakes at 3:00 or 4:00 am. Staring at the shadow patterns on the ceiling from the street lamp, he comes to see, at age 31, he's been scaling the wrong wall. This is an agonizing realization, this regret, which burrows between his ribs, festering like a sore. Now that he sits at the top of his fortress—good money in the bank, 28 full-time employees, two kids, a knock-out wife—his heart still feels kicked, a menacing voice in his head still shouts he's a lousy screw-up. The voice grows louder, won't quit. He's so goddamned sick of himself. He's heard the lingo on this kind of crap—mid-life crisis. But, this is more like all hell breaking loose. Hard as he tries, Benjamin Barrens can no longer contain the blasphemous truth—the chronicle of his childhood.

Part Two

Chapter Four

LELAND

LELAND BARRENS—WHO WILL FATHER BENJAMIN in five years—is 12-years-old when he starts twitching. That's what he calls it: twitching. It's almost imperceptible at first, but his mother, Frannie, sees it. His fingers make tiny, involuntary movements and his chin abruptly jerks to the left, as if his hands are occupied, while shooing a fly. A month passes before Frannie takes him to Dr. Arnold, although her husband discourages the visit. "It's growing pains—nothing that a good run outside won't cure. He's lazy, is what he is."

"Too bookish," is how Tom Barrens speaks of his son, when the boy buries his head in history books and likes, more than anything in the whole wide world, to peruse the maps in his *Fitzwilliam's Pocket Atlas*, naming the capital of everywhere and picking out Mumbai, Bangkok, Senegal, like the back of his hand. As a child unhappy at home, far-away places possess a special lure.

Had there been another boy—an athletic son—to distract Tom, Leland might have been left to attend to his scholarly pursuits in peace. But there is only Leland's older sister Dora, who doesn't interest Tom much, except to plot how to marry her off, which seems imminent now that George R. Rutherford is returning to Millers Falls.

. . .

A day so beautiful cannot be the bearer of bad news, thinks Frannie, as she sits next to Leland in Dr. Arnold's office, awaiting their 1:00 appointment. Mother and son walked the two miles into town, which felt like a treat to Frannie—forgoing the washing, ironing, and baking, at least for the afternoon. Yet, upon arrival, she learns that Dr. Arnold has been "detained," and as they sit waiting, the stillness and silence make space for her fears. Leland has been twitching more frequently over the past few days; he seems irritable and his color is sallow, subtle differences only a mother might detect.

Dr. Arnold's hand is pudgy and cold upon his greeting, after mother and son are ushered into the small, sterile examining room. Leland is instructed to sit atop the exam table, while Dr. Arnold takes a seat directly across from Frannie, who wonders why he hadn't thought to buy a new suit, as the one he wears looks at least two sizes too small, the jacket pulling tight across his chest, his pink flesh cascading over his shirt collar. Even his round, gold-rimmed spectacles seem too small for his fleshy moon face, leaving indents on his plump, flushed cheeks. While taking a formal history—scribbling several of Frannie's answers into a blue ledger notebook—the doctor's forehead begins to sweat, which Frannie worries is a response to Leland's prognosis, but rationalizes it's simply the doctor's incapacity to breathe in his restricted suit coat.

"We're all done for right now, Leland. You did a good job. Now it's time to sit in the waiting area while I have a word with your mother."

Has she heard of Huntington's chorea, he asks. No, she has not. As he takes a deep breath before continuing, a high-pitched ringing invades Frannie's ears and the dim room, curtains drawn against the sun, suddenly seems airless. She envisions grabbing Leland's little hand and walking straight out into the bright afternoon light, into the breath of the breeze. Tom was right—going to the doctor is silliness. She never should have come.

"It's a progressive, degenerative neurological disorder, Mrs. Barrens, characterized by rather abrupt involuntary movements of the muscles—in the limbs, face, hands. While it's an inherited disease, you have indicated no history of this affliction in your family or among your husband's relations. But as you describe, both your husband's parents died young, so they might, indeed, have been carriers yet to exhibit symptoms." The doctor wedges off his eyeglasses, pulls out his handkerchief and blots them dry. She wants to ask questions, but suddenly feels stupid beyond measure—unable to grasp the words *degenerative, neurological, affliction,* dropped like bombs into the stale air. But Dr. Arnold does not pause for speculation.

"Of course, as the illness progresses and unfortunately, no doubt it will, we can treat the youngster (*the youngster!*), with antispasmodics, likely hyoscine, in addition to sedatives. I like to use sulphanal. Be assured, Mrs. Barrens, I have expertise in this field." *A sales speech no less!*

Stop right there, she wants to warn, her wash-worn hands clenching her starched cotton skirt, her legs lead-heavy, but paradoxically poised to run. Does Leland's sister exhibit signs of the condition, he wants to know. *How dare he pull Dora into this? Outrageous!* she wants to scream, *Leave us alone! And then more!*

"Have you noticed mood changes in the boy—increased irritability, aggression, obsessive thinking?"

That June, Millers Falls' hottest on record, it is Frannie who obsesses, ruminating on the curse of this affliction upon her family, wondering what evil she's committed to deserve the wrath of God, reviewing her life with scrutiny and scorn. One might describe her as a God-fearing woman, motivating her to dress the family in their finest to attend Sunday services at Trinity United Methodist, for which she also volunteers on the first Saturday of each month, picking up soon-to-spoil fruits from local establishments to donate to those more needy than herself. Of course, she solemnly offers up her condolences to the Lord's forsaken souls, her chin lifted high to the heavens, mouthing, "There, but for the grace of God, go I." Her rapid and meandering thoughts turn to her next-door neighbor Flora Stapley, who she nursed back to health, almost single-handedly, mind you, even though the old woman's ratty terrier rampaged her garden the previous spring, for which Flora refused to acknowledge or repent. What did God think of her nursing facility and healing talents under such duress? Hmph, apparently not much. Has she not already had her fair share enduring the past five years with Tom, which she can only describe as too much to bear, her lips pinched as if she bit a lemon wedge—losing his job at the factory, at Christmas no less, having to seek money from his brother Carl, who wouldn't part with a pretty penny. And with Tom too along in years, anyhow, to be building the Futzwagger's new barn and it only a matter of time before their every last cent is spent. Frannie considers time and circumstance no friend of hers, thank you very much. How will she and Tom afford the doctor's bills, she frets—and with the results only treatment, not a cure? Even low doses of the antispasmodic make Leland catatonic, drifting off to sleep mid-sentence and showing no appetite even for his favorite supper—glazed pork chops and apple sauce. Yet, without the medicine, his gait becomes a stagger, looking positively drunk like Frank Malice walking down Main Street after stumbling from Bengotti's Bar, his legs buckling from under him, his whole body arching, then swaying.

At summer's end, Frannie meets with Claire Davenport, the school principal, who advises an at-home tutor, but how can they afford one? Surely, Mrs. Davenport has resources within the community, but she has none.

"Does the family have relations who might lend a hand?" *Is this her only advice?* Frannie doesn't want to reveal her family's misfortunes...her younger sister Lily with an illegitimate child and a full-time job, her mother, who died a year ago July, now resting next to father, headstones side-by-side.

Expulsion from school is the final blow to little Leland, who can no longer pretend to be like the other boys and girls. Frannie attributes her boy's bad temperament to his long days spent idle at home, but it is also the manifestation of the disease itself, which seems to have grabbed him by the ankles, knocked him to the ground and kicked out every hint of him. Dr. Arnold had warned of irritability and aggression, but Frannie cannot imagine these sour traits in her sweet son, until Leland intentionally flips his plate of mutton and mashed potatoes onto the dining room rug, carves the devil's face—horns and all—into his writing desk's varnished finish with a kitchen knife, and kicks the locked bathroom door off its hinge, scaring

Dora out of her wits, although, admittedly, she has a habit of dallying in there beyond any reasonable hour.

It is Tom who first utters the unspeakable: Mill Valley Insane Asylum—in nearby Worcester—couching the horrid intrusion of the word "insane" with "temporary residence," as he and his wife of 19 years lay side by side in their small bedroom, a stub of a candle, about to extinguish, casting a flickering light across the coverlet.

"Leland's not crazy," Frannie protests, thinking no one from their family would ever wind up in the crazy ward. "What are you thinking, Tom? I'm not putting my son in a place like that."

"I'm just bringing it up as an idea, is all," he says, knowing full well that Frannie will object. "You know Frank Mallory, the new foreman?" Tom continues. "He told me these places is more like a refuge, he called it, 'insane' just a word for people who have some kind of big trouble like a sickness they can't cure, or too much on the bottle. Frank's cousin was with syphilis, real bad, and got sent there." He pauses for Frannie's refusals, but her silence encourages him to carry on. "Frank says there's mostly old folks there that just lost their marbles."

Awake all the previous night seeking some kind of recourse, any recourse, to no avail, Tom reviewed the repercussions of his family's predicament, knowing full well that George Rutherford would break the engagement with their Dora if he discovered the family lineage marked by illness—inherited incurable illness—and with such a dreadfully incapacitating course. *Would the Lord deem it sinful to put the boy in a place where they could care for him, to keep him out of sight for just some time, just until the marriage is consummated?*

Dora's recent correspondence from George indicated his return to Millers Falls the day before Thanksgiving, and also intimated his intention to ask for her hand in marriage. It isn't so much that Tom likes George (in fact, George can be an ass), or that Dora seems sweet on him (how Tom hates his daughter's blushing descriptions of George's false valor), it's that George Rutherford has money, and maybe lots of it, down the road. Tom sees this as his family's only saving grace with the mounting medical bills, his wife's nervous state—already taking in more sewing than she can finish, and his own advancing age for his skills of menial labor. And what if his

21

own genes hold the horrid curse? What if Dora's body is coded for disaster, simply waiting—a week, a month, a year, to turn her existence from daydreams to nightmares?

"Utter foolishness. Nothing further from the truth," Frannie retaliates when Tom promises that the Lord won't test her more than she can bear, as she folds Leland's cuffed trousers and places them atop his balled socks, his starched and ironed shirts, his *Fitzwilliam's Pocket Atlas,* then locks the small trunk. Tom made the arrangements the previous Saturday, two weeks prior to George's holiday arrival, taking the four-hour carriage ride to meet Dr. Fletcher, the director, and tour "the sanatorium," as the good doctor deemed it, after Frannie finally came around, Tom offering repeated assurances of "temporary measures."

For the few days prior to Leland's departure, Frannie oddly distances herself from her boy, rather than, as one might suspect, fusses about him, making the impending blow more endurable for them both, she has contrived. She spends her days in bed, propped by two pillows eating stale biscuits slathered with butter and jam, rather than hurrying about the house in her usual fashion, picking up every small item out of place, double-starching the crease in Tom's pants, dicing the potatoes in regimented rows, tackling one more item from her basket of sewing. With the objectivity of a scientist, Frannie observes how quickly disarray sets in, entropy a greater force than will. Dora picks up a small bit of the cooking and housekeeping, but spends her idle hours sewing a new petticoat from the fabric of an outgrown summer jumper, in anticipation of George's arrival.

Omitting the proper name of Leland's destination, for fear he might outright refuse his fate, Tom offers assurance to his son that his "short stay at the hospital will help him get healed." In his head, Tom has convinced himself of this. In his heart, that is another matter, but fear of survival can do strange things to men, including severing them from sympathy of any kind, even for their kin.

Part Three

Chapter Five

SECRETS

BALTIMORE BOASTS SEVERAL FINE clothing establishments, but Cynthia, Barb and Colette enjoy casually mentioning to their wider circle of friends that their new outfits are from New York. Twice each year, the three coquettish women (Cynthia the blond, Barb the brunette, and Colette the redhead), board the 6:40 am Amtrak bound for the more sophisticated city to the north, beginning their highly anticipated day with breakfast at Lord & Taylor's third floor café, ritually ordering Earl Grey tea, fresh-squeezed orange juice, and Poached Eggs Hollandaise, which comes atop crust-trimmed white toast. The spring line has just arrived, and Marielle, the top salesgirl in Women's Better Dresses, hangs an A-line, yellow-and-white floral dress with a white patent leather belt on the curtain rod of Cynthia's dressing room in one size smaller, "to accentuate that wonderfully small waist," she commands with complete authority. Barb and Colette slip in and out of their own selections in adjoining dressing rooms in a not quite hurried but certainly steady pace, to make it to Saks Fifth Avenue, too, before boarding the 4:00 pm back to Baltimore.

It is often well past 10:00 pm, sometimes as late as midnight, before Ben comes home from work, blaming his absence from family dinners on "emergency meetings" or "manufacturing complications." Indeed, the business is rapidly growing, new contracts come in weekly, five new employees were added to the payroll in the last quarter alone. The tire empire percolates with expansive energy; in contrast, Ben's energy contracts and recoils. He's lost more weight, his once full face now drawn, his once clear eyes now distant and faintly bloodshot peering out atop gray crescent moons.

Home alone in bed, Cynthia sees a short clip on the late evening news of the old Brayton Hotel leveled by a burst of dynamite, slowly caving in upon itself in a graceful, seemingly willful surrender, its architectural splendor cascading beneath billowing dust into rubble. The short segment that follows showing the town fire trucks surrounding the structure, their high arcs of water descending on its flames, almost provokes her tears. To numb her senses, she pours another splash of scotch atop the mostly melted cubes of ice in the tumbler by her bed and falls asleep, make-up intact, in her bra and half-slip, sprawled atop the black-and-white striped taffeta bedspread.

If not in a drunken slumber, Cynthia might have heard Ben mount the stairs, then Celia's cries, although they are muffled by the hot palm of his hand firmly pressed against the child's small, parted mouth, as he fingers her with his forefinger, pumping her faster and faster, until he comes in a convulsive release. Ben stumbles into the master bath, pushes his stained undershorts deep into the clothes hamper and crawls into bed. Hearing Celia's crying, Maggie ascends the stairs and rocks her back to sleep. Before returning to bed, Maggie closes the small crack of the window, hearing the wind rustling the leaves, foretelling an approaching storm.

Witnessing the scene from above, pacing, wringing her wrists, her white silk robe trailing behind in undulating waves like a tumultuous ocean, Lady Kamara brandishes a blazing thunderbolt and hurls it to Earth. A thunderous boom lights the cobalt sky. Mounting her white steed, she gallops across The Golden City of the Sky, over the Rainbow Bridge, to the Garden of Eternal Springtime, where she weeps until dawn. A copious rain falls upon the Earth's oceans in the blue-black night, the only witness restless sailors and the half moon. Lord Myran finds her seated beneath the towering white birch.

"How will she endure it?" Lady Kamara sobs. "Our daughter has not yet earned caution," she laments. "She should have sought our permission for this incarnation. She is reckless and impulsive."

Holding her close until she calms, Lord Myran replies, "And where, my dear Ladyship, did she learn these traits?"

Chapter Six

SELF-PRESERVATION

WHILE MAGGIE ATTENDED SCHOOL on and off and only through the middle of the tenth grade, she possesses intelligence beyond her education and 19 years. She runs the Barrens household with relative ease—preparing and serving each meal, cleaning the almost 5,000-square-foot house (although Wilson comes every Thursday for the "hard cleaning"), and caring for Vivian and Celia—all facilitated by her organizational skills and intuition. As Mr. Barrens begins to deteriorate and his downfall takes its toll on those around him, most notably his wife and children, Maggie seeks a strategy to keep the good ship running and primarily, hold onto employment. Her desire to preserve her job at all costs prevents her from fully attuning her sensibilities to Celia's plight. And no self-preserving black woman, in 1960, would accuse a white man, no less a wealthy and therefore powerful one, of messing with his kin. If she were to take another job, she concludes, where would she obtain a reference of any kind? And would another housekeeper, in their right mind, do any better and sound the kettle? No indeedy, she concludes.

Maggie slathers diaper cream on Celia's red and raw genitals to soothe the skin from the insertion of her father's fingers and then, as the late evening interludes progress, his phallus. The purple bruises on Celia's chin and neck from the hard hand of her father to muffle her cries are explained away by rough play. Almost blurting out the truth, Maggie bites her lip when Mrs. Barrens expresses irritation at the breakfast table about the late night wailing from a child who, with little exception, had slept through the night.

Cynthia, having relinquished the care of her children to the domestic help, denies her husband's aberrant behavior through her far distance. But like most wives, who possess an antennae-like attunement to all matters, particular sexual, of their spouse, she knows not the exact, but the near nature of what transpires in Celia's bedroom. Confronting Ben, nonetheless, no matter how tactfully, scares her. She fears his wrath; she fears shredding the net beneath her own comfortable existence, so the activities behind the closed door to the pale yellow-painted nursery, which transpire nearly nightly for more than a year, remain lodged there, concealed in the dark. Keeping his secrets turns out to be a relatively simple matter for Benjamin Barrens. Celia, not yet two, cannot verbalize her assaults, and Vivian, who at the age of four can already talk up a storm, is mercifully spared any such attack.

Chapter Seven

BLUE MOON

IT IS ON A CLEAR, UNCHARACTERISTICALLY WARM Tuesday in late February, as if the tranquil and pleasant weather flashed a mocking smile, that violence erupts, forever altering the lives of the two women at the stately house at 1322 Grant Avenue and the two small children deriving safety there.

It was easy to obtain a gun. Ben placed an order through the Sears Roebuck catalog that regularly came to his office, the only prerequisite having turned 21-years-old, and awaited its arrival through the United States Postal Service. He chose the Sentinel 9-shot .22 revolver because he liked the blued finish. He chose the three-inch versus the five-inch barrel, for he assumed he could more easily conceal it. He retrieved it from a recently rented post office box, specifically obtained to discreetly receive his purchase.

Waiting until the last of his office staff leaves for home, Ben unwraps the square cardboard box and extracts its contents. The smooth handle fits well within his hand. The weapon easily slides into the inside pocket of his blue blazer. An assessment from every angle, carefully scrutinized in the full-length mirror in the men's room, reveals no detection of the weapon in his suit jacket pocket. Who is the man looking back at him? Ben does not know him, in fact, does not remotely recognize him. As he stares at the stranger, it is harder and harder to bring his mind to just one thing; his thoughts fly fast, squawk and flap like a flock of wild geese, and then scatter. Resting his sweating palms on the cold edge of the wash basin, he slumps over the sink, shuts his lids against the blaring light and tries breathing deeply to steady his thinking. It's five nights now that he's had no sleep. Linda, in the front office, having gathered the courage, asked if everything was OK at the end of the work day. She didn't want to pry or make trouble for herself, but it only felt right to show concern.

"Why, Mr. Barrens, I'm on my way. All I was saying…I was just wondering if, well, there's anything…"

"I said, 'Go home.'"

If he had one wish, he'd command his mind to stop. Thoughts of the past, present, and future race and reverberate in his head. Sitting in the driver's seat, his back stiff and straight, his Cadillac the only car in the office lot, he turns the ignition key to muffle his mind by the radio, but the announcer's tone is authoritative, accusatory, in condemnation of Ben and Ben alone.…*the report recommending troops to pound the National Liberation Front… fighting in the territory to the north.* He turns the radio dial, the small yellow bar sliding down through the hiss and static, skipping past the garbled phrases of blaring advertisements…*big blowout…family-owned and operated*…the car suddenly filling with the excruciating sweetness of song…*Blue Moon, you saw me standing alone, without a dream in my heart, without a love of my own.* Quickly cutting the volume, Ben drops his forehead to the wheel, his thin body convulsing in sobs. He feels for the metal beneath the silk lining of his jacket, ignites the engine, makes a left out the lot—the front and then, the back wheels rising and releasing over the high curb—and heads for home.

Chapter Eight

TWO POLICE CARS

MAGGIE WAKES AT DAWN, not by Celia's customary piercing cry, but by the sun alone. *He done gone and suffocated that child*, is her first thought. "Lord Jesus, forgive me," she pleads in a whisper, as she mounts the stairs. Stopping short at the landing, she takes a breath, bows her head and gestures the cross. As she turns the knob, then swings open the door to Celia's room, the little girl stirs and uncurls. Maggie mutters, "Thank the Lord." Standing over the crib, the morning cold, Maggie repositions the blanket, tucks it in at the sides. Only minutes later, the morning coffee not yet boiled, she hears the rapping of the knocker on the front door and sees two police cars out the kitchen window. While almost frantic, before she answers the door, she checks for Mr. Barrens' car in the garage. It is gone.

...

At Brock Avenue, nine miles from home, Ben drove past the Fillmore Hotel, its circular drive lighting the night with a regimented row of old-style street lamps, like a necklace of jewels. On impulse, he U-turned and pulled into the side lot, thinking of the hotel bar, where he had, on occasion, chosen a call girl for a rendezvous in an upstairs room. The anticipation made him grow hard, the longing in his loins pulling his energy down from the unceasing jabbering in his head. He imagined mounting her from behind, the small of her back swooped low, a shudder, a release from this world.

At the end of the dimly lit oak bar, a brunette, her short hair teased high, sat nursing a drink, her long legs descending to black high heels resting on the shiny brass foot rest. Aside from a young couple engrossed in conversation at a candlelit cocktail table, the room was empty, even the bartender was gone. Ben stood at the opposite end of the bar waiting to gauge her face since it was turned…to consider her. She lifted her heavily lined eyes, shifted her chair toward him, pushed forward her chest, then morphed her pout into a false smile in an attempt to appeal, but it was her solitary sadness, her vulnerability, that enticed him to take the seat next to hers. Her low-cut beige blouse revealed the rounding of her breasts. He wanted to bury his head there and sob. Her long fingernails, painted mauve, played with the uppermost button of her blouse. She asked if he was from out-of-town. He didn't answer, but retrieved his money clip and placed $100 in her lap.

Unable to climax, Ben collapsed atop her back, in exhaustion, in anguish. His sobbing scared her and she was grateful when he uttered, "Leave." Alone now in the dark room, he dressed slowly and methodically. Seated in a high-backed wing chair, Ben placed the cold barrel at his temple, hooked his finger around the trigger, and pulled.

The Baltimore Sun
Early Morning Edition
Wednesday, February 25, 1962
Benjamin Barrens Shot Dead Apparent Suicide

Benjamin Barrens, 31, President and CEO of Atlas Tire, was found dead at The Fillmore Hotel of an apparent self-inflicted gunshot wound late Tuesday evening, according to a report released by the Baltimore County Medical Examiner. Martin Smite, Chief Investigator at the Baltimore County Police Department said, "There are no suspicious circumstances. Everything points to suicide."

Mr. Barrens' assets were estimated by this newspaper, in January of last year, at $3.2 million. His truck and automobile tire company, Atlas Tire, Inc., headquartered at the Carnegie Building, 550 East State Street, Baltimore, which he began with $1,700 and a two-year loan from Franklin First Savings in 1951, was rated the fastest growing company in Maryland, 1956 through 1960.

Lawrence Nigels, assistant manager at the Fillmore, who was summoned to the hotel's third floor at 10:40 pm, Tuesday, when Mr. Harold Gossett in a nearby room called the downstairs desk to report hearing a gunshot, is making no statement at this time, except to report that the hotel will reopen tomorrow, when the investigation will be finalized.

Mr. Barrens leaves behind his wife of eight years, Cynthia Jayne Barrens, and two daughters, Vivian, 4, and Celia, 2.

Chapter Nine

BRIGHTER SHADE OF BLOND

CYNTHIA'S REPOSE THROUGH THIS ORDEAL and for months that follow is attributed to her nightly drinking, by which she blunts her senses, but the more accurate explanation relies on her lack of heart. She doesn't lie to herself that she loved Ben, yet his last few months roused loathing. How she abhorred his anger, his lashing out, his condemnation of anything and everything she did or said. Her thoughts immediately go to money. *Will I have to work? How much is owed on the house? How much is owed in the business?*

The following day at the accountant's office, she pulls her chair a bit closer to Leonard Sutkin's highly polished desk, smoothes her skirt, and politely asks, *"Exactly* how much is there?" When Cynthia's fears are more than relieved—for her late husband's debts are minimal and his investments in real estate (in Maryland and New York), nearly match his multimillion dollar business assets, and life proceeds, more or less as it has—she decides changes are in order and buys more youthful clothes and dyes her hair a lighter and brighter shade of blond.

For Celia, her father's death brings repeated assault and terror to a swift and miraculous halt. Yet, the psychic scarring remains ingrained, its concealment in shadow creating a force more damaging than if revealed by light. When she grows to become a peculiar child, no one pays much notice, since she is strange with regard to too much, rather than too little, compliance.

"What a good girl she is, your Celia. Not even one tear!" praises Dr. Evers, the pediatrician, holding the empty hypodermic needle.

When the chicken pox encrusts Celia's scalp and blisters under her arms, Cynthia remarks, somewhat puzzled, "She never complained."

The child's stoicism stems from her inability to feel much of anything—pain or joy—for she has developed, as most children do of misuse, an ability to remove herself from herself. The human body, even in the littlest of forms, is uncannily equipped to conjure tricks to numb the hurt, to keep alive. Terrorized, with her father looming large, Celia learned to turn her head ever so slightly to the side, the white slats of the crib marvelously fusing to a solid sheet of light into which she merged. From this protected space, off to the side and hovering above, she watched the scene with curiosity, with what one might even describe as wonder.

Had she ascended higher and higher still, Celia might have faintly heard Lady Kamara's distant murmurings, uttered in a dream, an imagined homecoming, a vivid vision of her daughter's safe return in a crystal carriage led by winged black stallions with emerald collars sweeping through the cerulean sky—a spray of stars and moon dust trailing behind.

Chapter Ten

FRESHLY ICED

A S A RESULT OF INCREASING CONCERN for the curiously well-behaved child and regret for not having intervened, Maggie takes Celia under her wing. The nanny's new devotion is also encouraged by gratitude for a Lord that saved her from what she perceives as a close call by her master's hand. The year that Maggie turns twenty, she intends to make the most of her second chance.

Maggie reaches down to grasp Celia's pale palm, as they cross Gaton Avenue, heading back for home. In her other hand, she clutches a cotton bag filled with fresh fruits and vegetables. On Saturday mornings, with little exception, the plump nanny in her white uniform and the rail-thin, wispy-haired blond, (whose small size foils strangers into guessing her age at two or three, rather than her proper age of four), make their weekly trip to the farmer's market. Sunday mornings mean that the kitchen fills with the smell of cinnamon-and-sugar sprinkled apples bubbling within a browning crust, and sometimes a peach or cherry pie, too, whichever fruit is in season before the market closes for the summer in mid-July.

With Maggie's help, Celia sifts flour and rolls dough—a limited participation, but enough to elicit pride in the young baker as Maggie opens the oven door, hands encased in well-worn mitts, and like a miracle, pulls out the finished product.

"I made that," Celia always glows, then sits by the kitchen timer set for ten never-ending minutes of required cooling before Maggie will cut her a slice and remark, "Well, just this once. Lord knows, it'll ruin your lunch, but we gotta put some meat on them bones."

While Maggie teaches her numbers by counting things aloud ("How many here?" before cracking three eggs against the side of the large glass bowl), she isn't much good at reading, so story time means paging through the Scriptures, with which Celia becomes enamored, beholding the strong, but tranquil faces of the winged angels on the glossy, heavy-stock sheets like gifts between the sheer pages of text, left unread.

Most of all, Maggie becomes a mirror reflecting Celia's sentiments, and in this way the child comes to faintly recognize herself, to distinguish her own feelings. "Why so sad?" Maggie asks, when Celia pouts. Or "Heaven have mercy, go put those cold tootsies in some socks," Maggie scolds. And in this way, Celia stirs deep inside, mustering something solid by which she holds herself straight. Her stomach aches less and she puts on weight. However hesitantly, it seems safe for Celia to take up a little more space for that happy year—a year like a sweet dream of wishes fulfilled, where deepest longings are met—until Maggie starts to drink.

At first, Maggie steals sips in the afternoons from the Missus' liquor cabinet, but soon stashes her own bottles of whiskey beneath her bed, of which Celia is aware. As Celia grows, she conspires with Maggie's frequent tales of headaches and backaches that draw her nanny to bed in drunkenness, anger and despair. Seeking to rouse her caretaker and lost companion, Celia brings Maggie iced coffee with an extra-big scoop of vanilla ice cream, massages her feet, keeps a freshly iced washcloth on her forehead, and plays her favorite song, three or four times, carefully lifting the needle back to the second selection, Side B, *Amazing Grace*, until the spell might break and Maggie might sing along, her crossness finally gone— for now. These drunken bouts become nightly events. In this way, the two survive Celia's childhood.

...

Like many young American women morphing their identity to encompass the country's shifting ideology in the sixties, Cynthia Barrens undertook her own metamorphosis, shedding her persona for a seemingly more liberated role. After dating an artist ten years her junior, who captured her flesh in muted tones of pink and gray, and then a restaurateur of an upscale steak house (fourteen years older), who kept her intoxicated with fine wines paired with prime rib or grilled shrimp, she settled into a relationship with the debonair owner of a successful cruise line, Leo Mastinni, who wore custom-tailored cashmere suits and ascots made of the finest silk. For nine months of each year, they sailed from port to port on international seas, where Cynthia liked to linger, when docked, in small boutiques and luxury resort gift shops, directing accommodating retailers to airmail her purchases home. For Vivian and Celia, she bought exuberantly expensive clothing in sizes too small. Occasionally, an outfit gift wrapped and assigned to Vivian was Celia's right size, although Celia never had the occasion to wear, for example, the silk-lined tweed skirt and suit jacket with the matching cap, or the pleated, ankle-length ivory velvet dress, hemmed with embroidered lace. Maggie stored these outfits, plus outgrown clothes, in boxes in the basement. Cynthia's packages often contain short notes of endearment (*Mommy sends xx*), scrawled in loopy script on large royal blue envelopes, stamped with the ship's insignia, enclosing an 8-inch by 10-inch photograph of Cynthia and Leo seated at the Captain's table; the ivory linen littered with glittering crystal candlesticks, ashtrays and wineglasses; Cynthia, in a strapless dress showing off her slender, tanned shoulders, her highlighted hair parted to the side and swept up.

Cynthia's excursions abroad begin by boarding the plane in Baltimore, then catching a connecting flight to Barcelona or Rome, thereby whisking her away from the hissing whispers of housewives in supermarket checkout lines and the idle talk over bridge tables on Friday nights. Suicide, as Cynthia soon found out, carried a longstanding stigma of sin, which increased in proportion to Benjamin Barrens' wealth. The news of the tire king's death disseminated as fast as the speed of commuter trains on which weary nine-to-fivers, their newspapers held close amid the clamor of the morning rush, read the front-page story in disbelief, then settled into wondering where the hell they were racing if this was, after all, their pie in the sky.

The fallout hit the Barrens girls, too. Vivian's name was erased from the invitation list to Teresa Mullen's birthday party at Wilcox County Fair, that spring—the only second grader not in attendance. Celia frantically chased Suzie Seem, her best friend, around the cracked concrete playground at kindergarten recess, as Suzie's mother had forbid her daughter to play with Celia from then on, quickly staging after-school playdates with "those other nice girls in your class."

Vivian and Celia are unaware of their plight, having no clue of the suicide and its aftermath. Dr. Evers, the pediatrician, deemed it wise to tell the girls a tale, suggesting to Cynthia that the suicide be attributed to accident.

"An accident of what type?" Cynthia softly inquired in Dr. Evers' office. The two discussed varied scenarios in pleasant tones—perhaps an accident at the tire plant, an airplane crash, a car crash, a calamity involving great heights, say a tall ladder, say broke his back, all the while, the good doctor trying to stay on task though prone to distraction, tracing the graceful curve of Cynthia's prominent collar bone as she primped just a bit, pushing her blond hair back from her neck. It occurred to them both, in somewhat awkward fashion, that Cynthia's status had suddenly shifted; she was no longer the property of the powerful Benjamin Barrens, but a single woman, quite available. Cynthia liked the car accident best and told the girls that a taxi driver hit their father's car and he was instantly killed. There was an emphasis on the word "instantly," the descriptor signified a merciful act.

Children who experience loss or abuse become hypervigilant and Celia is no exception to this rule. If bad things happen out of the blue, it makes sense to keep an eye out, in the hope of dodging trouble. In some ways, this serves her; it's a useful tool. Here is a child who doesn't miss a beat, at home or at school. She is an attentive student, paying heed to her increasing responsibilities, as she grew. Yet, while all seems fine on the outside, on the inside, she does not exactly bloom. She is more an artificial flower, lacking life force, her existence serving for the sake of ornament. From this child, one hears no laughter or even a sigh of relief, no temper tantrums or even a tear, as if the exultant "me" and obstinate "no" are obsolete. She is neither hot or cold, hungry or thirsty, tired or wired. Since the abuse occurred before she turned three, compartments within her memory flitted away as she grew. She has no recollection of her father's nightly attacks. None at all. So Celia's sorry secret remained sealed in a time capsule, until she conjured a special voice, the language of the mute, who speak through action and often lack thereof, replicating the crime and their victimhood. In this sad and strange way, she became her own perpetrator, as well as prey.

One of the earliest indications of this roundabout expression is evidenced in her relationship with her first love, Erik Engle, who sits at the desk in front of hers in American History, junior year, fourth hour. Erik is a pretty boy. He has long blond hair, so neat and straight it looks blow-dried. Sometimes, he ties it in a ponytail with a braided leather strap. This is 1975. Through the first semester, Celia stares at that silky hair. Like the popular pretty-boys of the day, Davy Jones and David Cassidy, Erik's petite physique and feminine features appeal to girls who still feel safer with girls. This is true for the adolescent Celia.

Erik Engle wears the same green army jacket every day, without exception. This jacket makes him cool, although he can't be classified as such, meaning he's not in Tommy Bano's clique or anything. Nor is he a greaser, a jock, a pothead, or a preppie. If he has one designation, it's poor—he lives east of the Brook Crossing industrial plants, by the train tracks, a smidgen of diversity in the otherwise upscale zoning that carves out the student body of West Woodlawn High School.

Erik lives with his mother in a third floor apartment, with no washer or dryer. She was hauling his duds to Swift 'n Clean Laundromat, however this underappreciated service recently came to a sudden halt, his mother hoping to give that boy some responsibility of his own. A real pity is how Erik saw it, especially since he dropped a whopping dollop of meatball hero sauce straight down the front of his beloved army jacket, which wouldn't dab out with a sponge. Also wearing, by rotation, the same 14 pairs of dirty socks and underwear for nearly two months, he intends to clean his clothes and salvage his prized coat.

A boy senses when a girl stares at the back of his neck throughout history class, so he swivels in his seat, quite cavalier, and asks Celia to hang out. "Hanging out" is pretty close to a date. Of course, Erik calculates the locale of this date at Celia's house, where household appliances surely whiz and whirl. He knows she's one of those Madison cul-de-sac kids—the area's wealthiest enclave. He doesn't exactly hate Celia, for he's never heard her utter a word, but he hates kids like her, who are stuck up and spoiled.

This date happens the following day after school. Erik thought of stuffing his old backpack with his soiled clothes and bringing it along, but assessed he'd have to wait another week, maybe two at the most, for a full-service afternoon. This is a sweet deal for Erik Engle, who gets what many guys vie for, but must offer something in return. While his beloved army jacket tumbles dry, he's working his way to second base, pushing at the seam of his jeans to make room for a rock-hard boner. Celia is flat-chested and only sort of pretty, but nonetheless, these perks come with access to the refrigerator and pantry from which Celia extracts two flavors of ice cream, Pop Tarts and Ring Dings.

"You must be pretty hungry," Celia says, her lips and chin chapped and puffy from too much rough kissing. Erik doesn't regularly shave and his faint stubble has grown in. They're sitting at the kitchen table. He's ripping the cellophane wrap off his fourth Ring Ding, leaving one in the box, having relinquished the pint of Vanilla Swirl, after working his way down to a half-inch covering of ice cream over the wax. A fleck of chocolate icing hangs from his left nostril, which Celia finds especially endearing.

"Did you finish that stupid assignment for Mr. V?" asks Celia of their history paper.

"Shit. We have to hand that in tomorrow. Lemme see yours, so I can get some ideas."

Celia doesn't want to show Erik her homework; she says, "Sure."

An awkward silence makes Celia shift in her seat, but she can't think of anything to say. After an excruciatingly long pause, she mumbles, "I think you're cute." She's hoping for an admiring reply, but doesn't have the nerve to look, so she drops her chin, her stringy blond hair falling forward, shielding her face.

"I hate the word 'cute.' Do you have any more of that licorice?" he asks, getting up, looking in the cabinet by the sink.

Celia is in love, for two-and-a-half weeks, before she sees Erik making out with Tracy Horton behind the high school cafeteria.

Directing her energy to the cluster of brayberry twigs and sinta seeds, Lady Kamarad lights them aflame. Seated before the fiery alter, she bows her head and sings. Next, she takes the sharpened horn of the Crytaliton and in one swift stroke slices off her four-foot braid. Her glossy black hair, now shorn at her chin, falls like a dark curtain over her tear-stained face. "I offer my body and soul to hasten your return," she summons, laying the thick black tress atop the blue-tipped flames.

When Vern Grimalski, who picks his nose in math class and has crusting acne around his mouth, asks Celia to go the movies that weekend, she feels a wave of revulsion and then, nods yes. In the backseat of his rusted aqua-blue Pontiac at Dusty Point, she pulls down her jeans and to Vern's astonishment guides his aching member inside. His effusive gratitude gives her a glimmer of power, but she quickly pushes that feeling aside, as the primary purpose of the act is a penance she's dealt herself, although she isn't sure why.

Celia is puzzled by kids having fun in high school…joking at the bus stop, going to parties, joining the track team, getting a part in a play. Even more bewildering are those seemingly destined for despair, who appear not simply resigned to, but actually OK with the whole nightmare. How does Nancy Grossman get out of bed each day and hoist herself up on the bus? Celia guesses she's over 350 pounds—not just overweight, but seriously obese. Yet, she seems content; had a boyfriend sophomore year. And what about brave Liz Macknimee in a wheelchair after the bicycle accident? She laughs at the lunch table with her friends and started that handicapped club. When Celia sees their smiles, she hates herself for her own bitterness, unhappiness and loner status.

As if a theatergoer viewing a play, Celia takes in the plot and the dialog, but never participates on stage. She is a voyeur, seated in the dark. Like some out-of-the-ordinary kids, who spend too much time alone in adolescence, she turns to art. Art is her escape, her longed-for relief. She turns off, crawls out, with paint. She likes paint, everything about paint…the smell, the texture, the vast variety of colors, the way it globs on and drips off a brush. She goes to galleries and museums to look at paintings and to art stores to buy supplies. She pushes her bed to the far wall of her room and sets up an easel at the window. That corner of the earth becomes her sanctuary.

What does she paint? Awful stuff—rainbows and flowers made with tiny, tight brushstrokes on oval-shaped canvases. This has to come out before other stuff can come through. Her color palette soon morphs from spring greens and sunny yellows to Cobalt Blue and Mars Black. She buys large canvases and begins slathering it on. The concentration that the craft requires takes her away from herself. It hushes up the hateful self-talk in her head. The larger canvases are mostly abstract. If pressed to point out something recognizable, there might be a woman's face or a place where the sky meets the sea, but mostly it's just shapes and paint…paint for paint's sake. There's some anger there, too, in her vigorous, painterly style, as if a barely audible voice finally piped up, hissing *take this, take that.*

On Saturday mornings, Celia boards the 10:25 am bus headed for the city to The Baltimore Museum of Art, leaving the suburban streets for the cacophony of car horns, the rumbling motors of buses, the men and women crossing the busy streets, walking the crowded sidewalks. She revels in the frenetic pace and the anonymity she finds there; she doesn't have to hide behind a canvas pitched in the corner of her room, yet she disappears. Her "art bag," containing her customary stash—spiral sketchbook, two charcoal sticks and a small pack of pastels—is slung over the shoulder of her navy blue pea coat atop faded and fringed Levis and sneakers—standard attire at West Woodlawn High. The genetic code that formed her mother's exquisite face did not line up for Celia, but she has appeal, nonetheless, with an angular jaw and a small, straight nose, (like her father's), and eyes the color of sand (like her hair), with a hint of the sea. She's ghostly pale and much too thin, possessing a malnourished frame, but accentuates her narrow hips with a suede belt with fringe; even post-sixties, the hippie style predominates for teens. Characteristic of self-conscious adolescents, she does not stand up straight and like a sapling barely rooted, she appears not firmly planted. A sudden gust of wind might lift her skyward into thin air, soaring toward clouds, then vanishing like a lost balloon on a string.

Word got around school and after confronting her mother, Celia learned of her father's suicide. Nearly numb, she has little recognizable reaction to the critical news. Sometimes, she thinks her father courageous to have taken his life. Sometimes, she stops in the museum gift shop, where she buys posters that, one by one, plaster over the pale yellow of her bedroom walls. It requires a certain amount of psychic energy—the cover-up of the crime, the suppression of her father's assaults.

Following her Saturday afternoon excursions to the museum, Celia fulfills Vern's fantasies in the backseat of his mildewy Pontiac on Saturday nights, until Rick Danzinger appears on the scene. Rick has an apartment downtown, a perpetually shiny Datsun 280Z with coconut air freshener that smells like the beach, and a Tony Orlando mustache.

This turn of events might have been an opportune time for intervention from a family member. Maggie had been the child's mother in every practical sense, yet she was let go when Celia turned ten. Cynthia left Leo Mastinni that same year, their liaison fast-deteriorating when he turned up a wife in Madrid that he refused to divorce. The event brought the puffy-eyed Cynthia back home to Grant Avenue, but only in physical form. The breakup hit her hard and she immediately took to bed, cucumber slices atop her lids, a scotch by her side, the television turned down low, so that only the booming pitch of commercials and the shrieks of canned laughter in sitcoms were audible at her locked door. Wilson came twice a week to clean the house and cook chicken stew. In the winter of the following year, Cynthia took a lover—Larry Fox, recently divorced, who owned a car dealership. Vivian, two years older, had already left for college. It might have served them both if the girls were close, but neither child possessed a capacity for support. All in all, therefore, this is to say that Celia had no guidance or supervision.

Rick Danzinger is 26, an even ten years older than Celia. His hair is wavy and dark and he wears it shagged and parted on the side. His body is small and compact and he dresses neatly and always gargles with mouthwash. He has a thing for blondes and younger girls. He's in his father's business—building supplies. Lazy at work and a womanizer, he's set up his days so he can loaf around and get laid. He has the city pegged for pickup spots. Beyond his favored parks and cafés, he occasionally does the museum, looking for new material. One Saturday afternoon, he starts up a conversation with Celia. He wears a black turtleneck with a brown corduroy blazer, dark blue jeans that fit just right, if not a bit too tight, and black cowboy boots, recently polished. Celia feels him looking at her. Most people, upon a glance in his direction, would not have noticed, as Celia does, the gold ring with a black stone on his pinky.

She senses his approach from the other side of the Modern Art room. He stops next to her, in front of a Jackson Pollock painting. This makes her heart beat so hard and fast, she thinks he might hear it pounding. She's so uncomfortable, she begins walking toward the next painting on the wall, but he catches her in conversation.

"So, watcha think? You like it?"

"Um, yeah." She's thinking she's a moron for her short and stupid reply.

He smiles at her. He has good teeth and a sexy smile. He knows it and uses it. "Why didn't I think of it?" he attempts a joke. "Open up a can of house paint and pour it out. I cudda been rich and famous. I'd get a discount, too. I mean on the house paint. I own my own company—real estate development supplies." Celia stays silent, too nervous to speak. He adds, "I'd rather look at a painting of you. You'd make a pretty picture." Her pale skin blushes pink and she lowers her chin.

"Tell me what you think of this one." Here, he touches her elbow, every so slightly to guide her left. It's a tiny touch, but unmistakably charged with seduction. They stand before a painting by Francis Bacon titled, "Seated Woman." The agonized subject sits on a dismantled couch, hunched over, her legs contorted, her feet grotesquely pigeon-toed.

"Oh, I love Francis Bacon," she says, aiming to emphasize her knowledge. "His work is so, well, raw." She looks up at him, hesitantly, through her strings of blond hair, for an affirmation to her reply. He flashes his smile. It's a sinister grin, but she takes it as an acknowledgment of her sophistication. He asks her out for brunch, sensing he's hooked a live one…Dorian's Greek Café, the following afternoon.

Arriving early, Celia nervously sits on the red vinyl couch in the entryway next to a fountain flanked by oversized faux terracotta vases sprouting dusty plastic flowers. Watercolor scenes of Greek landmarks, yellowed behind smudged glass in gold frames, line the walls. A standing screen separating the back room displays a distorted-perspective painted scene of the Parthenon. By the cashier, she eyes a bulletin board with tacked-on Polaroids of zealous customers seated at tables and below these, framed black-and-white publicity photos of Bob Hope and Telly Savalas, and a head shot of a man with a pained smile, tacked to the wall with a push pin, that she tries to recognize—a local newscaster, she thinks.

The juke box above the nearest table displays in bold red type: *Silly Love Songs*—Paul McCartney and Wings; *Don't Go Breaking My Heart*—Elton John and Kiki Dee; *Take the Money and Run*—Steve Miller Band; *50 Ways to Leave Your Lover*—Paul Simon. Piping in overhead, she hears *Jive Talkin*. Below, on the speckled Formica table, a bud vase with a brown-at-the-edges red carnation swoops over a rack of Sweet n' Low. The sun pours through the half-shut peach-colored Venetian blinds, bent at the ends, making it stuffy and hot. She takes off her coat and folds it neatly atop her lap. She straightens her back.

He's wearing so much cologne that Celia smells Rick before she sees him standing behind her. It's a cheap and spicy smell. He bends down and gives her a kiss. She can feel his thick mustache and then, his moist lip. *I can't believe he likes me*, she thinks. His display of affection boosts her confidence and her stomach settles.

The sour-faced man at the cash register slides two huge, glossy menus under his arm and hastily leads them to a booth in the back. Rick takes the seat facing out. Once settled, Rick's agenda—to navigate a non-circuitous route to bed—is artfully crafted around casual questions, nicely spiced with half-assed compliments, as they order and eat their sunny-side-up specials. He smothers his with ketchup. "I'd never guess you're still in high school— you look like a college girl to me. So, no boyfriend? Of course, you must have had quite a few…I can tell when a girl is sensual. You are. What school do you go to? I bet you're a top student."

While fielding this pop quiz, Celia notes that Rick is color coordinated, a theme around the black of his hair and mustache. Beneath his lightweight V-necked black sweater peeks a powder blue and black paisley-patterned collar. A gold chain with a small onyx and gold cross hang over the sweater—this coordinates with his pinky ring. His keys, placed on the table, have a matching ornament. These items were purchased as a boxed set. His eyes are deep brown, almost black. His gaze, unabashedly, is aimed at her chest. In the parking lot, he stands an inch from her face and asks if she'd like to see his place. Even after eating, his breath has a hint of spearmint.

Rick is a rote lover. It is, however, this part of his practiced repertoire that ultimately places Celia dangerously within his control, under his thumb, so to speak, or one might more accurately say, "thumbs," which when held side-by-side and moved quickly, give Rick good technique. Going "down there" with his tongue is considered "unclean," he tells her. So, Celia douches with products touting *spring fresh* and *floral scent*, but to no avail. A different brand with a fragrance called *strawberry style* makes her smell like a fruit salad. Still, nothing. She later understands that the cross of Jesus on his bedroom wall had more to do with it than what he called her "fishy smell," the corners of his moustache curled low beneath his frown.

After two weeks using condoms, Rick demands that Celia "take care of it," so she takes the bus to the Planned Parenthood clinic, where a doctor in training, under the direction of a physician apparently not directing, fits her with a diaphragm the size of the yarmulke Jacob Steiner wore at his bar mitzvah. Several sizes too big, it gives Celia a whopping infection, and to Rick's dismay, Celia closes shop for the weekend. Mysteriously, Rick is suddenly busy with projects at work on Saturday and Sunday.

When she returns the following Wednesday and finds travel bottles of girly shampoo and conditioner in his shower, he's adamant that there isn't someone else—and this is true. There were two girls. Twins. Celia doesn't buy the story about a cousin visiting from Virginia, but doesn't know how to prove it.

Red in the face, he says those exact words: "Prove it," then, pours himself a scotch. After Celia showers and leaves the towel on the rack not exactly straight, he descends into rage—his apartment having to be kept just so. She doesn't understand Rick's system of haphazard orderliness. In the center of the kitchen table, for instance, is a mound of yellowed receipts—

from restaurants, gas stations, and drug stores, piled two-feet high. And inside the frig, sticky rings of goo stain the shelves and black moldy blobs, like hairy monsters, grow in the fruit drawers. The bed has to be made a special way, too—like Celia's in the army or something, but Rick doesn't wash the sheets, which are black silk with crusty cum stains and smell like sweaty socks.

Often, Rick's displays of rage are strategic—meant to intimidate. If Celia admits her fear of his infidelities, he lets her know her jealousies are prohibited. This works. Celia never says a word. She doesn't really want to catch him, anyway. That would entail ending it and, of course, she loves him. She buys him presents to show her affection, watches cooking shows and then, makes him gourmet dinners wearing lingerie—he likes black lace. One Sunday morning, he asks her to clean his apartment in her bra and panties. While on her hands and knees scrubbing the kitchen floor, he watches and jerks off. She looks up to see his face contort when he climaxes and revels in his uttering her name. She's wanted, needed. He loves her. She does, however, experience a twinge of degradation. This lowly position, her nose at the floor, feels oddly comforting, as if being spanked, but knowing it's deserved.

She is needed in other ways by Rick. When he gets frustrated with his father at work, she consoles him. If he seems tense, she massages his feet. She's good at that. If he brings home paperwork from work, she sits with him and helps him. Love poems for her beloved are penned in perfect script within handmade cards, which keep her busy at night, often at the expense of her homework.

On the inside of her locker at school, she taped a Valentine's card he gave her. He had to go to the drug store to buy it, while she waited in the car, but he signed it, "With Love" and picked one out that said, "The most precious thing that a man can have in this world is a woman's heart." Celia thought the cover was pretty corny, though: a photograph made fuzzy of a couple holding hands walking in a park. The girl had brown hair and was dressed sort of womanly in a skirt and high heels, but the guy looked a bit like Rick because he had a mustache.

···

It is the week following this romantic holiday that Rick's indiscretions turn up certifiably undeniable, Celia's visit unannounced. Her stride from the bus stop to his apartment is quick; it is windy and cold, the sun hidden behind the tall buildings, taking its descent before dusk. Celia lifts the collar of her pea coat and digs her hands in her pockets for warmth. Tucked under her arm, meticulously gift-wrapped, is the new album by Hot Tuna, released that day, which she bought at Denny's Music Den, downtown. It's Rick's favorite band and she's decided to surprise him that Tuesday— fearful that he'd buy it for himself by Friday night—their next date.

The couple is leaning against a car—his hips pressed against hers—in front of his apartment house. The girl laughs and throws her head back a bit. The guy nuzzles in and kisses her neck. Celia almost walks right past them—she doesn't recognize Rick at first, because he's wearing some kind of stupid ski hat. Oh, how she wishes she didn't stop in her tracks, aghast, two feet before them, the record album falling to the sidewalk.

"Shit, you scared the hell out of us. What are you doing here?" Rick shouts, facing Celia now, feet in a wide stance, knuckles pressed at his hips.

"I can't believe…how could…you're such a liar," Celia says, feeling the blood rushing to her cheeks. She runs down the street fighting tears. She doesn't want them to see her crying. Ducking into a Burger King on the next block, she locks herself in the restroom. Standing in front of the mirror, she watches the tears stream down her cheeks, black with mascara. *You're ugly as sin*, she thinks. *No wonder he doesn't love you.* She expects and relishes this shame, this rejection of her love. She isn't meant for happy or happily-ever-after. That's for Karen and Nancy, who giggle in small clusters at the lockers, who walk hand-in-hand with the tennis team guys—Ken Wentworth and Tony Spire, who go to prom with pearl necklaces and corsages, their fathers wondering where the time has gone, their young daughters suddenly young ladies slowly walking down the carpeted stairs.

It's now dark and sleeting, the ice falling on her face like darts. Celia walks south, past the warehouses, inviting trouble, seeking complicity with her feelings of worthlessness. It is the wet weather that protects her—the vagrants are off the main streets, sequestered in tunnels and alleys, huddling before flaming cans for comradeship and warmth. Walking toward home, her ears freezing, her feet aching, she's shelling out punishment for a rotten, naughty girl.

Something elemental shifts that night. In her relationship with Rick, Celia reenacted her father's abuse and is sunk by the force of the original assault. It is a pain she could not survive as a tiny child, and here, it almost sinks her, but not quite. A kind of ghost arises that functions as Celia at home and school. She has a dream that night that she is on a ship that ignites into flames. There is pandemonium. At first, she fends off the frightened crowd that pushes her aside seeking safety. Then, her perspective shifts, she lifts up; sees herself from above. Suddenly, she loses track of herself. She can't pick herself out from the crowd and vanishes into nothingness.

The radio alarm blares. A branch of the large elm outside her window raps the pane, the rain pounds. The announcer reports highway hold-ups: *Tractor trailer accident—avoid the Wilmont exit…rain and sleet continuing through Wednesday.* Most mornings, a sickening song sounds: *Boogie Oogie Oogie, Copacabana* or *Candy Man.* Fuck Candy Man. *Who can take a sunrise… sprinkle it with dew…cover it with choc'late and a miracle or two… oh, the Candy Man can. The Candy Man can 'cause he mixes it with love and makes the world taste good.* Celia flings her arm overhead, hitting the alarm off, and opens her eyes. An excruciating reality descends, as she catches sight of the text books strewn across her desk. From where does she summon the will for her first small acts of the day—sitting up, putting her feet on the floor, rising for school?

That Saturday, a large package arrives from her mother, staying at The Pierre Hotel in New York—with Larry Fox. It's a raccoon jacket. Celia feels that this ridiculous extravagance should not be relegated to the basement and tosses the coat in the back of the car. She heads to the warehouse district in her mother's Lincoln Continental. Double-parking at the once gilded entrance to The American Hotel, she steps out and gives it to a prostitute leaning against the ornately carved door. "I hope it keeps you warm," Celia says holding out the coat. The woman snatches it, in case the crazy kid might change her mind. Her eyes are bloodshot and yellowed and lined in too much black make-up. Parted in the middle exposing a streak of dark roots, her hair is greasy and thin. A red patent-leather raincoat is belted at her waist topped by a pink, dirty scarf looped around her neck. Clutching the fur close to her chest, tears welling in the saddest eyes Celia has seen, the woman whispers, "Bless your heart."

That night, Celia flicks on the fluorescent light and marches down the basement stairs to find the other never-worn and outgrown clothes that her mother mailed over the years. After organizing them into sizes in the morning, she puts them in the backseat and trunk and drives to the donation center for The Salvation Army.

. . .

The following week, Celia decides to forgive Rick, her dearest beloved, for his indiscretions. Curled in a fetal position on her bed, the phone at her ear, she announces, "Hi—it's me, Celia."

"What's up with you?" he replies, his tone angry.

"I just wanted to talk. I miss you."

Rick misses Celia, too—the way she looks from behind in her panties.

"So, come over."

After sex, with Celia's face resting on his chest, she strokes his arm and says, "Are you still seeing that other girl?" She holds her breath. Rick knows he should come on strong—he isn't going to put up with this bullshit. He likens it to bad debt—the last slot on the spread sheet. You write some of it off. You have other paying customers.

"Nobody ever said you were the only one. We're dating is all," he replies, rolling away from her to the other side of the bed, running his hand through his hair. "Who gave you a ring anyhow? This is the way things are." He thinks, maybe, that sounds too harsh. After all, he wants to have her once in a while. He likes her ass. "Don't I please you in bed?" he adds for good measure. Celia starts to cry. She tries to mask it, but he can feel her tremble.

"You do. Of course, you do. I just don't know why you need to see someone else. What does she give you that I don't give you?"

"She doesn't complain like this—she knows how to have a good time."

"But, I'm fun to be with….and I help you with things."

"Who asked you to do shit for me? Don't do shit just because you want something back. That's selfish." Celia starts to really cry now. "If you're gonna get all cry baby about it, you should go home."

"Home, indeed," commands Lady Kamara, "to The Golden City of the Sky, to your parents, who yearn for your safe return." It had been 17 years since she held her dear daughter, born from the iris of her eye, her birth the gentle release of one tear—a tear of joy. Yet, Celia grew to be fire instead of water, air or wood. "Fire is beautiful, but dangerous," Lady Kamara advised her young child, who possessed a rebellious spirit from the start.

"A voracity that won't be controlled," Lord Myran would say, shaking his head side to side, when Celia retaliated against all rules they put forth. Hence, her celestial parents view her earthly station not only with heartache, but with bewilderment—at how submissive and lacking in spirit she's become. As the years pass, it is harder for them to remember the fiery spirit and courage that impelled their daughter to accept her earthly assignment and they fear her getting lost in the illusion of separation from source, prolonging her return home to the celestial plane, mired in a myriad of successive Earthly incarnations.

Her mission on Earth, as decreed by Council in the Book of Books, reads thus: Transform the psyche of Celia Ann Barrens from subjugation to power. If her assignment shall be sealed with the silver stamp of victory, her transmutation helps propel empowerment to all womankind—as the universe is an interplay of connected energetic forces. Reinstating matriarchal love and compassion provides a restitution of Earth's delicate balance. Yet, this metamorphosis of her spirit demanded a precondition of Celia, a ruthless command resembling a riddle. It was summoned that all skills gathered from eons of fighting the forces of misogyny be wholly relinquished. The battle was to be fought without mystical insight, without spiritual sword, as if sending a sightless soldier to war.

Celia sobs so hard, she barely can see the road. Once home, she pricks her pinky with a pin and spreads the drops of blood on a blank page of her sketchbook, smearing in script, I love you Rick. At her easel, she lays out her palette of paints in a semi-circle, like a necklace of multi-colored gems.

Rummaging through the tubes in her paint box, she unearths Cadmium Red, squeezing a generous dollop among the varied hues. Red becomes a predominant color in her paintings that year, a symbol for anger, pain, and blood, an expression of her thwarted love.

Celia dares to imagine that her recent paintings might be good enough to gain her admission to School of Visual Arts in New York City. She envisions the abundance of world-class museums and their promise of inspiration, the bustle of the big city and her anonymity there. When she receives the formal letter of acceptance, her hope is restored and her destination is determined—she will move to Manhattan. Across the bottom of the letterhead is scrolled: *You can paint—we hope you'll join us*, then a sloppy signature she deciphers: Harlan Lee Wolfe. She immediately looks up the name in the school catalog; he heads the painting department.

As part of her father's estate, her mother inherited two Manhattan brownstones. When Richard Togin's one-year lease expires that August, Celia moves into the building on Ninth Street in Greenwich Village, walking distance to the school on 26th Street and Fifth Avenue. That summer, she imagines things opening up for her, taking a turn for the better, in a new city, in a new home.

Chapter Eleven

NEW YORK

NEW YORK ENABLES CELIA TO BE a little more like Celia. She doesn't feel so many unwritten rules around her. She cuts her hair—straight across, just above her chin, ditches her worn-out Keds and sixties-style peasant shirts and buys a few vintage outfits from a thrift shop, a few blocks west of her apartment: a black velvet fitted jacket with a leopard collar, a crushed-velvet Bette Davis hat with an antique rhinestone pin on the brim, several fitted silk blouses, and a hot pink wool jacket, short and flared with three oversize black buttons. Watching old black-and-white movies has enamored her with the styles of the forties and she gets an added kick buying clothes that cost a few dollars. She wears her finds with jeans and red, high-topped Converse sneakers, walking with more bounce in her step, even with her large, black portfolio swinging in her clasped hand and her overloaded backpack weighty with art supplies, on her way to and from class. Wearing no other make-up, she often makes her mouth a deep, matte red. This brings out the porcelain quality of her skin. A fashionable woman on Fifth Avenue stopped her to inquire where she bought her "marvelous handbag," which she'd purchased at a flea market—

a small box purse in red patent leather trimmed in black feathers with a short bamboo handle.

Her new home, her two-story brownstone, seems to her a palace. The upstairs becomes her painting studio. Downstairs, she has a small kitchen and bath, and a bedroom that faces a tiny courtyard. Her furnishings are sparse and also acquired from rummaging thrift shops and frequenting varied vendors on Broome Street on the first Sunday of each month.

Celia's favorite class is art history with Dr. Anne Applegate. The classroom is always dimly lit upon arrival, the only light emanating from a slide of a painting projected on a screen at the front of the room, while the students file in and take their seats. Celia loves the colors and composition blown up big like that, Dr. Applegate sharing tidbits about the artist's personal struggles, and analyzing the times in which the artist created. It's both thrilling and intimidating to Celia—these legendary works of art. It occurs to her, seated before the oversized images projected on the screen, that art is a pretty strange endeavor. A painter spends long hours before an easel, honing tricks—often turning three-dimensional reality into two-dimensional form to express something about reality, just the same. Why, she wonders, does she want to devote herself to this circuitous means of communication, where the gist of the matter is expressed so indirectly? If truth be told, she supposes, it exists beneath the surface of things. If truth be found, it resounds beyond intellect, reaching the soul. This seems, on the whole, a worthy act. Yet, it also strikes her as indulgent, this luxury of solely immersing herself in the area of study of her choosing, no longer having to endure science and math, as she did in high school. She half-expects an authority figure—a tall man in uniform—to tap her shoulder and say that she get on with "the official program," by promptly returning her attention to bilateral equations and the wingspan of a fruit fly.

While college life provides opportunities for Celia to make new friends, she largely remains a recluse. After attempting to have fun at parties, as well as throwing one of her own, and joining group outings to nearby restaurants and clubs, she declines further invitations. There's a lot of drinking and slurred speech, and stupors are a reminder of her childhood. Socializing doesn't come easily to Celia. Yet, when she isn't painting or studying, her single status does not prevent her from exploring New York.

Taking the Fifth Avenue bus uptown, she often visits Central Park Zoo, watching the monkeys swinging on vines, the seals honking and clapping their fins in a corny show involving slippery fish as treats for tricks, and a white polar bear pretending he's a swimming star behind thick glass. Her favorite is the baby orangutan nestled in her mother's reddish-brown fur. As much as she wants to be a sophisticated *artiste* surveying the varied facets of culture in New York, this little ape is the highlight of the city. She has a soft spot for baby animals and looks leisurely and adoringly at calendars of kittens—sitting in teacups and curled in tiny baskets on sunny windowsills—at a nearby bookstore, before perusing the coffee table books in the art section. Thursday nights and Sundays are spent at the Metropolitan Museum of Art and the Modern Museum of Art, where she lingers before magnificent artworks. Late into the night, she paints, infused with the power of masterpieces. Her paintings are improving and Harlan Lee Wolfe, or as the students call their teacher, The Wolf, takes note.

"Big stuff coming from little stuff," he says to her in painting class, as she reworks the upper-right quadrant with a lighter shade of blue. She turns to see him towering behind her—a big man, his square jaw cocked to the left, resting on his balled fist, his eyes assessing her painting in slanted slits. "Looks like you've been soaking in some Rauschenberg," says The Wolf. "If you're taking something from another artist, little lady, then *take* it. *Steal* it. Make it *yours*. Don't replicate." This startles Celia, for she was enamored with Rauschenberg's paintings that past Saturday at the Museum of Modern Art. *How did he know?* This both scares and impresses her—The Wolf's uncanny perception. He steps closer to her back and whispers, "Come talk to me after class." She feels his breath on her neck.

"Come in, come in. Take a seat," The Wolf motions toward a chair facing his. The small room is dimly lit, the blinds slightly cracked, so that bars of shadow stripe the paper-strewn desk. A life-size skeleton, sometimes used in drawing class, stands ominously in the corner, its black eye sockets staring out. The Wolf wears a purple button-down shirt streaked with drips of paint—the multi-colored lines forming a web. His washed-out jeans are also paint splashed. There's a rugged sexiness about him, his thick gray hair falling in waves around his angular face. The bridge of his nose is too high, but straight. A diamond stud earring, on his left lobe, flickers in a shaft of sunlight. His hazel eyes are piercing and Celia feels him look right through her. This unnerves her. She feels she can hide little or nothing from him. She sits straight, her back rigid against the chair. Nervous, she smiles pleasantly feigning a relaxed state.

"Tell me about Celia," he says, lacing his fingers behind his neck, pushing his chair back, so it rests at a steep angle against the wall, positioning himself to fully focus on assessing this new student of his—the most promising in his freshman class. He picks them out at the beginning of each new year, circling around them like a vulture flying closer and closer in. Celia senses a constriction in her chest, her palms go wet. If only she could slip straight out of her seat and disappear. She's stripped of her protective shield—the mask she often wears in the world.

"She wants to be a painter," she replies. "At least that's what I've been told. It could be a lie. I guess we'll see." This makes The Wolf laugh. Pushing his chair straight up now, he intensifies his gaze on her, rubs the gray stubble on his chin with the back of his hand—his lips pressed together like he might be pinching a toothpick there—one of those manly gestures that naturally come to him.

"Why paint?" he asks.

"Why not?" she says, trying to evade him.

This makes him laugh again.

"I like you, little Celia. Let's have lunch."

And so it began.

Chapter Twelve

THE WOLF

S HE BERATES HERSELF FOR FUSSING about what to wear. She's meeting The Wolf at a health food restaurant, a couple of blocks from school, a hole-in-the-wall juice bar and salad spot, where no one goes. Maybe she won't feel him towering over her with a little extra height, she thinks, drawing high-heeled black boots under her jeans. Carefully pulling a fitted black sweater over her head, a vintage forties cashmere with black beads sewn around the collar (snagged at a flea market for two dollars), so as not to muss her hair, she then, wraps a red silk scarf with beaded fringe loosely around her neck and applies Beat Red, her signature lipstick. She recently cut bangs, late one night before the bathroom mirror, after watching a Louise Brooks movie on TV, and this 1920s bob shows off her eyes and makes her look a bit older.

She's never seen The Wolf off campus, and as he sits before her, it feels more like a date than anything else. He parks his elbows on the edge of the small table, so he can rest his chin on his palms and stare. He's a sponge, soaking in what pleases him, drinking it in or storing it away for future use in his artworks. He says nothing, his silence intended to intimidate. They know him there—the cook behind the counter and the waiter—and they fix him up fast with "the usual." To initiate Celia into eating what's "alive," he tells her, he orders her what he's having…a tall glass of wheat grass, parsley and celery juice, with a shot of bee pollen. They share guacamole and chips and a plate of glistening grape leaves stuffed with spiced brown rice. It's tasty, but Celia takes birdlike bites because of her fluttering stomach. The Wolf touts his health regimen and Celia guesses he's aiming to keep himself young and virile with his vegetarian diet and seemingly fanatical exercise programs—25 or more miles of jogging a week—an attempt to slow Mother Nature. *How old is The Wolf, anyway? Too old for you*, she thinks. *This is the kind of guy that makes your knees shake*, she concludes.

"Suburbs, right?" He asks, swinging back the last of his drink, popping a grape leaf into his mouth.

"What do you mean?"

He takes a long time chewing and then says, "You grew up on a tree-lined street. Daddy's a doctor. Mama cooked meatloaf and mashed potatoes."

Harlan Lee Wolfe hates the rich kids and pegs them, each year, from the get-go. Besides the clothes and the car, they have all the most expensive gadgets and supplies, and of course, as a prerequisite, no talent. The scholarship kids are often the better artists. Celia intrigues The Wolf because she doesn't fit the mold. The Wolfe family had little money, his father sunk by The Great Depression. He attended Rhode Island School of Design on a full ride. An incredible draftsman, he excelled in a realist style.

"Almost right," she says. "Baltimore. Big house. Fucked up family. No mashed potatoes."

He smiles. He wants to hate her, but he doesn't.

"Not living in the dorms, then, huh?"

"I'm on Ninth Street. I have a great working studio—good light and space."

"I'll show you a great studio," he says, throwing a few bills and some change on the table, yelling back to the waiter, "See ya tomorrow, Barry," and standing up. Celia quickly rises to her feet and they walk around the corner—he lives on the next block. It's an old, small apartment house, falling into disrepair. The lobby, with faded floral curtains, a worn beige velour love seat, and two fake ficus trees, smells like cigarette smoke and bleach. The elevator door creaks open, shaking on its tracks, and he pushes five. There is so much sexual energy in that tiny, rising box, Celia thinks it might explode. The hall is narrow and the door is painted a thick, ugly brown. He fiddles with the key and swings it wide.

Celia is stunned. It's like entering a whole other world—a universe onto itself. The walls are a shiny, deep red and lined by The Wolf's large paintings—nudes of women. Celia has only seen a few of his paintings in books and catalogs, but the small reproductions do these grand works of art no justice. The painted female figures, while realistic, are stylized. Bold blues and yellows, as well as stark whites and blacks, brilliantly beam against the blood-red walls. A corner window pours in light, a northern exposure. Here, he has two large easels and steel shelves of neatly stacked supplies— paints, brushes, and jars of paint. Lush plants, some flowering, in huge black and tan pots, frame the windows. Overgrown spider plants hang low from ornate hooks in the shapes of animals. Standing African sculptures— mostly of women, their bare breasts carved from smooth brown wood— are interspersed among the foliage. *A jungle*, Celia thinks. Gauguin in Tahiti, she imagines. On the floor, lays a young woman, nude, her brown hair in a bun, a silicone or maybe a resin sculpture. At first glance, Celia thinks the sculpture is a real person and she jumps back in fright. The Wolf laughs. This is a joke he plays on all first-time guests. It never fails to amuse him. Celia recently saw a show of similar hyperrealist sculptures at a 57th Street gallery.

A cat emerges, meowing, and brushes up against Celia's boot. Squatting down, she strokes its back.

"That's Frida Kahlo," he says, surprised that his finicky Frida approached someone new. He scoops her up with one hand, reaches high and places her atop a tall, antique, mirrored armoire, where the black cat sits noble and erect, like an Egyptian statue. On the left-facing wall, a framed poster announces an exhibition of his work. The large print portrays a reproduction of one of his paintings, a female nude, and below, in elegant script: *The Paintings of Harlan Lee Wolfe. September 17 – October 22, 1952. The Women of New York Series. Paul Booth Gallery. 19 East 57th Street, New York.*

Celia calculates fast: 26 years ago. She knows the story well—everyone at school knows. The Wolf hit it big early on—right out of school. There was, and remains, no better art dealer in New York than Paul Booth. But The Wolf's fame and success were short lived—three years—before the realist style was fully shelved, making way for the new artists of the day, the Abstract Expressionists, who deemed painting reality, whether a nude or a bowl of fruit, utterly and inexcusably passé. The Wolf was still signed with Paul Booth Gallery, but rumor had it, Booth only sold his paintings to a diminishing group of collectors. Prices, most notably at auction, plummeted. Refusing to ride the tide, Harlan Lee Wolfe still painted the female nude. He was and would remain one of the top figurative artists in New York, but almost no one bought his works. Begrudgingly, he finished up his master's and took a teaching job at School of Visual Arts. Celia guessed that the collectibles (African sculpture and masks, and art glass), and the pricey antiques (gilded mirrors, intricately carved cabinets, the crystal chandelier), decorating his apartment, were relics of an earlier, more prosperous era. She didn't know if it was just a rumor, but had heard he sold his penthouse on Central Park West when he couldn't make the mortgage. She'd also heard that his falling status drove him to drugs, and ultimately to rehab. It broke up his marriage. It was all true.

"This one's a former student of mine," he says, pointing to one of his paintings—a nude portrait of a beautiful brunette—her wild, curly locks falling atop her small breasts, her eyes staring out at Celia. The Wolf places his hand on the small of Celia's back and stares hard at her for a response.

"It's a powerful portrait," says Celia, skirting his intentions. She feels flattered, but also terrified, her stomach turning, the grape leaves and green juice threatening a repeat appearance. She quickly changes the subject. "What are you working on these days?" making her way to the easels, where a charcoal sketch, the rough beginnings of a new painting, outline a reclining woman.

"I'm working on inspiration," he says, sarcastically.

Flustered, Celia announces she'll be late for art history class if she doesn't get going. She thanks him for lunch and closes the door behind her. Riding the elevator down to the lobby, her stomach flip flops; she thinks she might throw up. It would serve her if she learned to listen to her gut.

On her walk back to school, a cold wind picks up, refreshing her. A late November afternoon, it rained the night before—an all-night downpour—and the air is crisp and cool, as if out at sea. How she loves the urban beat of life around her. At the corner, waiting for the light, she watches a bearded man with a bounce in his step grasping a bouquet of daisies; two beautiful men—dressed like models—walking hand-in-hand; a group of punk rock kids slinking by in long black coats over laced black boots, laughing and passing a joint. On the next block, lemons, apples, and oranges, piled high in perfect pyramids at a grocer's stand look to Celia like sculptural works of art; and a young street musician having finished a long, lovely riff is packing up his saxophone. She reaches into her coat pocket, smiles at him, and slips a twenty in the case of his shining silver horn before he flips it shut.

"That was generous," she hears someone say, and turns to see Sloan Ford leaning against the side-entrance of the art building. This surprises her. Sloan has a reputation as a recluse and she hasn't heard him utter a word, all year, to anyone. A third-year architecture student, he's known for his avant garde style. Celia saw a model he'd made for an architecture show at the school gallery and thought the small replica looked more like a ship out at sea, with billowing sails, rather than a building. Even in his khaki cargo pants and baggy pullover fisherman sweater, Celia can see his slight, long frame. She pictures him finessing his architectural designs into the late hours of the night on sheer inspiration alone, forgetting altogether about food, about sustenance. She watches him tuck an intricately folded glossy sheet of red paper into his coat pocket, as he catches up with her at the school entrance and opens the door, ushering her inside.

"What is it?" she asks, of his shiny red paper.

"Oh, not much. Origami—you know, the Japanese art of folded paper. It's a bird. Here," he says, extracting the winged creature, about the size of Celia's hand—all details exactly as they should be…beak, plume, outstretched wings, tiny webbed feet. Celia involuntarily gasps. It's so beautiful. "I think this little chickadee has found her home. Will you take her…accept her as a small gift?" After marveling at the bird, turning her over and around, Celia looks up to thank him. Although his face is cast down, she can see he's blushing. He quickly turns from her and says, "See ya."

Celia yells down the hall, "Thank you. I'll take good care of her." She pauses and then says, "What's her name?" She wonders if he's heard her.

Sloan abruptly pivots and stands perfectly still, facing her now, over twenty feet down the hall. He thinks for a moment, smiles, and says, "Miss Celia." She didn't know he knew her name.

Without a moment to spare, Celia slides into her seat, as Dr. Applegate begins. Applegate is new to school, having recently completed her doctorate at Yale, then a teaching stint at Tyler School of Art in Philadelphia, before relocating to New York. Expressive with her hands, she waves them around (her silver bracelets jangling), in enthusiastic gestures, elucidating her passions for art and life. Celia listens attentively for Applegate's tips on living the life of an artist, often laced into her lectures. Applegate's class also is, on occasion, zany. Applegate's husband, a zoologist, received a clock as a present from a colleague, first tossing it into a hall closet and then attempting to throw it in the trash, so Applegate hung it in her classroom. In place of each numeral, the clock displays an image of an animal—a horse, a cow, a pig, and so on—and instead of chiming, it sounds the noise of the animal. These moos and oinks were set to sound at the full- and half-hour, but the clock busted and randomly blares the roar of a tiger or the meow of a cat at any odd time, humorously mocking or disparaging the speaker or subject at hand. That previous week, Applegate was sharing tidbits about Picasso and his womanizing, while married to Francoise Gilot, when the clock sounded the horse's long, loud naaaaahh. This broke everybody up. Celia watched Applegate smile, take a step back and clasp her hands at her heart, basking in the rich roar of amusement surrounding her. Celia had never known anyone who reveled in inciting delight. From that moment forward, Celia imagines that Dr. Applegate is her mother, setting out scrambled eggs and buttered toast for breakfast, her silver bangles glinting in a shaft of morning sun. Applegate would call Celia "my love," and inquire about their plans for the day to come. The ensuing day would be normal—so normal, it could be a TV show: a neighbor stopping by for coffee, laughter faintly heard in the kitchen while the women poured themselves another cup, grilled cheese sandwiches cut on the diagonal for lunch, a visit to the library—a mother and daughter excursion, father praising the picture she made in school—proudly tacking it on the wall.

. . .

The Wolf is absent from class the following week. Celia learns that his mother is ill and he's flown to Florida to see her. When he calls Celia that Friday afternoon, she's astonished. He hopes it's OK; the administrative offices gave him her number. He'll be back Sunday, he tells her. Can she retrieve some things he needs from school and bring them by that night? "Yes, of course," she says. She writes down his small list of requested papers and books and where to find them in the art room.

"Rough week," he mumbles. "It'd be a great help," he adds before hanging up. Celia isn't too young to see this as a set up.

. . .

It's windy and raining and she can't get a cab. There's no bus in sight. Celia walks the 16 blocks to The Wolf's apartment and when she arrives, even though she had an umbrella, she's soaked. Fortunately, she'd put his books and papers in a plastic bag and hands them over, dry.

It takes The Wolf less than an instant to suggest that she get out of her wet clothes. He gives her one of his button down shirts; she changes in the bathroom. It's white and crisp and comes down to the top of her knees, like a dress. She stands before him—her feet cold and bare on the wood floor, her wet hair matted to her face—as he cuffs each sleeve to her elbow with his big, tanned hands...slowly, too slowly. "There," he says. Celia wants to reach up and touch his hair, fold into his arms, be safe, warm and secure there. "Do you want tea? Let me make you something hot." She sits on his red velvet sofa, sipping tea, in silence. He sits across from her in a black leather chair. Anything Celia thinks to say, to break the quiet, seems silly and foolish. Her face becomes flushed from the steam of the tea; her red lipstick is still slightly smeared above her mouth, even though she wiped it off standing before the mirror in the bathroom. She looks like she's just been kissed.

"I want to paint you."

Celia lowers her head. Some part of her, deep down, understands this means trouble, but wrapped in that same thought, she understands she will pose for him. He half-stands, reaches over the coffee table, and with the tips of his fingers, arranges her bangs, so they fall straight on her forehead. She lifts her eyes to meet his. Her eyes say, *Don't hurt me. Love me. Take care of me.* Without saying a word, she says yes. The Wolf rises, grabs an antique wooden chair and sets it by his easel. He hurriedly circles the room assessing props, placing them near the chair. He turns on a large standing lamp and an overhead light and motions for Celia to take a seat. She isn't sure why, but she wants to cry.

"Don't be scared," he tells her. Reaching back to his stereo, he pushes the power button. A Mozart sonata, sweet and pure, fills the room, shifting Celia's mood. She begins breathing more deeply, while sitting as still as she can. Frida rouses, slinks over, and jumps onto Celia's lap. The portrait is instantly set: Celia, hesitant and longing for love, wearing a man's oversized white shirt, her lipstick smudged…atop her lap, a black cat. Sunday afternoons—a modeling schedule is tentatively set. Well past midnight, a working charcoal sketch intact, he takes her downstairs, hails a cab, and gently kisses her forehead.

. . .

The following Sunday, he suggests "a slight adjustment to the costume." The shirt should be unbuttoned to her waist and left slightly open. He explains that the portrait will capture Celia poised between childhood and womanhood. Standing before the easel, his long legs in black, paint-splattered jeans, his hand on his swayed hip, he assures her, "The shirt will still cover your breasts, although a purple shadow on the cloth will evoke your nipples." He walks to the window, adjusting the blinds to get the shadows exactly right, evaluating her presence in varied dark and light. "What I want to see is the bony chest between them and just the suggestion of the rounding of your breasts." He crouches before her now, slowly unbuttoning her shirt, his fingertips rough and calloused. "Yes, like that…an opening, an exposure." Next, he encourages her authentic countenance: "Will you look at me now?" He smiles, while straightening her collar. "What I want to see on your face, for the portrait's sake, is your wanting me. Imagine me less years, more money." He laughs, the self-effacing suggestion meant to relax her, for he already intuits her desire.

She lets the muscles of her cheeks relax. She licks her lips; her mouth goes slightly slack. She drops her chin—just an inch; her large green eyes look up into his. Nodding affirmatively, he places the palm of his hand on her cheek. The moment lingers too long and he pulls back from her, abruptly stands, turns his back and without a word, walks to the kitchen, returning with two glasses of ice water with thinly sliced, floating lemons. Beethoven pours out from the stereo like the sound of God accompanied by angels into the sunlit living room, while she sips the cold, tart water through a bright yellow straw. When she finishes, he takes the sweating glass from her hand, sets it down and begins with sweeping brushstrokes, laying in a watery wash of background hues. Frida, as if on cue, takes her place on Celia's lap. This makes The Wolf laugh—a deep, happy sound she is surprised to hear. At that moment, on a winter Sunday, she falls unreservedly for him, and he knows it.

A string of Sundays afternoons—thick with an electric sexual charge—follow, before The Wolf loses control. His kiss is not entirely uncalculated, however, for the portrait of Celia is mostly fixed. If things go south, down a rocky course, as he has experienced with his young models in the past, as he transitions them to bed, the painting requires only a few more sittings. Three or four romps in the sack are usually status quo before the delicate and pretty maidens expect more than he's willing to give. After all these years, The Wolf's art-making remains his main gig. He relies on the building of sexual tension—between the artist and his muse. It fuels his work. And then, like the cherry on the sundae, the last thing left, he dangles it above his mouth, engulfs it, and pulls off the stem. He eats it up, so to speak, in bed.

Celia has not yet had a real lover and she mistakes his lust for love. He is skilled at building toward climax, then receding, teasing her to want him. This goes on for hours and Celia goes home as if drugged and then, sentenced to a 10-mile marathon. Crawling into a hot bath, half-conscious—her arms held afloat by the almost unbearably hot water—she recalls their intimate moments…how he slowly traced her face with his finger and kissed the tip of her nose; that thing he did with his tongue in her ear—what was that? The way he covered the small of her back with kisses; how he adeptly turned her over or lifted her on top of him, abruptly changing positions. She replays, over and over, his moan of pleasure and his expression of painful surrender when he came—the lone, fleeting moment of their lovemaking when she truly had him, when she felt he wouldn't, couldn't, abandon her. What she doesn't want to think about, but it refuses to stop playing in her head, is the way he held her head down with both his hands. She thought she might choke on him; he pushed so hard and fast.

The secrecy that surrounds their forbidden liaison gives Celia an undisclosed power at school; she has another existence in an alternate world of which no one knows and many would disapprove. She magnifies this feeling by carrying, in the front pocket of her jeans, a smooth purple gem stone that belongs to The Wolf. One afternoon, while he was washing his brushes, she picked it up from a bowl on the living room window sill containing a dozen or so similar stones and slipped it into her pocket. During class, or walking down the hall, she reaches inside and holds it in her hand.

...

He calls her Friday night—just past eight. Can she come over if she isn't doing anything? She feels victorious—he can't wait 'til Sunday, their usual day. At his front door, he scoops her up like a child, lays her on his bed and undresses her. Afterwards, The Wolf is hungry and they order up vegetarian Chinese food, which they eat in bed, straight out of the boxes, with chopsticks. Entangled, they fall asleep. She has not yet spent the night.

It is not yet light, when he wakes her. He's had a bad dream and bolts up, sitting straight at the bed's edge, breathing hard, his brow and the back of his neck wet with sweat. He starts to cry and this scares her. She wraps herself around his back and strokes his hair; he lies back down in a fetal curl and Celia presses up behind him. "My mother," he whispers. "Nothing I do will ever please her." Lying awake until dawn, while he sleeps nestled in her arms, Celia envisions The Wolf opening up to her, revealing his heart, needing her support. She will console him, cook for him. Under her care, he will heal his deepest wounds.

He is awake, already at the easel, when she stirs. She sits for him while he reworks her hands and the shadows in the folds of her shirt. He scolds her for moving, but she could only be more still if she held her breath.

Often, they talk at these long sittings, but he works in silence and in anger. She knows not to bring it up and he does not say a word. Showing his vulnerability is against The Wolf's rules. He has broken his own code—a key self-directive—don't expose. He gives her money for a cab and sends her home. Overnight, it has snowed, but the dusting of pure white powder that covered the streets has turned to slush. It soaks her shoes.

During painting class, the following Monday at school, The Wolf stands behind her as she lays in some color and says, "You're overworking it. You know it looked better before adding all that Winsor green. Give it space. Come back to it when you're clear about the composition—about what you're trying to do." She wants to turn around and say fuck you.

The following Sunday, a cold February morning, he calls and says he doesn't need her to pose. "Well, let's do something else, then." Celia suggests. "What would you like to do?"

"I thought with final projects due in a couple of months that you'd prefer to study, you know, get your work done."

She knows she'll sounds needy. She can't help it; it comes out: "But, I want to see you."

The pause is too long. She holds her breath, shifts her gaze to the window. A bird perched on the sill takes flight.

"Celia, let's give it a rest." He hangs up the phone.

She tries going about her morning as if nothing significant has occurred. She constructs the day's plan. It's simple, a practical matter: *make a cup of tea, review my notes, finish the line drawing project, take a walk if it's not too cold.* Her steps in the kitchen feel oddly automated. Beneath her feet, the floor seems slanted, warped. She sits down at the small table, so distracted in thought, that the steaming cup of tea on the counter goes cold. She reviews the past months, making a mental list of her inadequacies, her faults. It's clear. She's messed everything up. She's a total fuck up.

In the bathroom mirror, she scrutinizes her face. Just yesterday, she assessed her reflection and found something appealing there. Today, she only sees imperfections. Her baggy V-neck nightshirt reveals her flat chest. In the center, between her breasts, she touches the small hollow space with the tip of her thumb. The Wolf planted kisses there, painted it in shadow with Caput Mortuum Violet, in her portrait. No one else will ever find it erotic—this little hole at her heart. She retreats to her bedroom, spends the day curled in a ball in bed, pours a bowl of Grape Nuts for dinner, which remains uneaten, hardening into cement, and sleeps two hours, after finally drifting into the relief of oblivion at 4:00 am.

How desperately she wants to stay home on Monday, but she won't let The Wolf know how deeply she's hurt by not showing up for class. She worries he'll continue disparaging her work, but he plays it cool, does not address her directly, scarcely glances in her direction. He's been through these break ups before, numerous times, and is intent on stifling negative repercussions for himself, most certainly within the environs of school. Dismissed now by the master of draftsmanship, the connoisseur of color, Celia produces little work. She packs up her station a few minutes early and goes home.

She continues attending classes during the bleak and bitter weeks of February and March, her Monday through Friday schedule a reliable and organized routine, a hook on which she hangs her languishing life like an old coat. Weekends are the worst—especially Sundays—dreaded Sundays. Sometimes she takes long walks, even if it's terribly gray and cold. Nearby, brownstones and side-entrances to apartments discreetly advertise the services of doctors and lawyers with gold-plated plaques on freshly lacquered doors. Several times, she stands before the door of Dr. Theodore Meissenhaus, psychiatrist. She looks up his number in the phone book and makes an appointment. Friday at 2:00. She almost doesn't go.

...

The waiting room is small and displays framed prints of Miró. *Scientific America* and *Smithsonian* magazines are stacked on the small glass coffee table. A wrought iron heater intermittently hisses and clangs, making the tiny room overly hot like an incubator.

"Celia Barrens, hello. I'm Dr. Meissenhaus, but you can call me Theo." He is a small man and older than Celia pictured him. In his sixties, she thinks. He wears a tweed blazer over a crisp, yellow oxford shirt. His hair is short and gray, the top of his head bald. His face is pleasant and freshly shaven—shiny and ruddy red.

Celia settles into a worn, beige leather chair across from his. It envelopes her in soft, cool leather. The walls are lined, floor to ceiling, with bookshelves, crammed with books. Stacks of journals overflow in piles around the room. A worn Oriental rug covers a scuffed wood floor. A vase filled tight with yellow daffodils sits in a spot of sun on his desk by the only window, blinds slightly open. He takes a small, brown leather notebook from a shelf and places it on his lap.

"Where should we begin?" he asks. "How can I help?"

Her gaze at her feet, wringing her hands in her lap, she says, "I guess, I'm kinda having a hard time at school." From there, the fifty minutes go fast. She is surprised that so much gushes out: her father's suicide, her move to New York, her affair and break up with The Wolf. The experience feels surreal—the mere idea of it—someone listening, really listening, and helping her put the narrative together as a whole.

Tuesdays and Fridays at 4:00. Celia strings her life around these magical hours, when she begins piecing together the fragments of her life into one increasingly clearer story.

By late spring, the school year coming to a close, The Wolf looks like a different creature. He's put on weight, just a bit, but it is, Celia thinks, well, disagreeable. A middle-age paunch hangs over the top of his jeans, which hug too tight now around his hips. He's grown a beard, which masks the strong, angular lines of his face. It makes him look older. It is the oddest thing. Not only is she no longer attracted to him, she wonders what in the world she was thinking. *Could this happen—this flip flop from love to repugnance? What exactly happens to the love? Does it still exist somewhere in the world? In a brown paper bag left on a bus? Will someone find it and eat it for lunch?*

This shift in her perception amends her ability to work. She spends more time in her studio. Her paintings have more grit. A mixed-media piece she made for a design class is chosen for exhibition in the school's year-end show.

. . .

That summer, in New York, Celia dedicates herself to excavating her childhood, eager for her twice-a-week appointments with Theo. He recommends several books that he hopes might elucidate the constructs in her family home. She devours them and finds more, headed home laden with bags from Barnes and Noble.

It is during these oppressively humid months of July and August, when the whole of New York is sticky and slow, that Celia becomes a reader, a voracious one. Why has she not accessed this Shangri-La before? She finds new voices—friends of her choosing, that open her world. She sets up camp that summer among the stacks in Psychology and Metaphysical. The basic conclusion: She is royally screwed up. First, there's this whole business with her mother, whose idea of mirroring, which Celia learns is essential to the child's formation of a strong self, means gazing at her own reflection while reapplying lipstick or evaluating her latest purchase from Bergdorf's. And, what about those abandonment issues stemming from her father's suicide? That's a thick-with-trouble case study, all in itself. She spends hours and hours reading about the lives of saints, the revelations of revered yogis, initially wondering what an old man wearing a loincloth on a mountaintop might offer, in terms of solace or advice, to a nineteen-year-old trying to make it in New York. But, once she lets go of judgment, she embraces the wisdom of their words and longs to access, however briefly, their world.

Broadening her selections and diminishing her costs, Celia gets a local library card and its needling sidekick, Mr. Late Fee. No matter what carefully calculated system of due dates she devises and revises, she falters in her intent of obedient citizenship. She reads until her eyes become watery and pink on her small patio in the early morning or at dusk in a ratty lounge chair she's picked up at the curb, her ankles spotted with mosquito bites. Overly air conditioned coffee shops house her new habit, where she sips tea with sugar and milk and nibbles a cinnamon scone. After a torrential downpour in early August, when the weather becomes tolerable, as if a fever broke, she takes a respite and rides the merry-go-round at Central Park, attempting to fill a hole in her childhood. She's never mounted a garishly painted carousel horse before. The warm wind on her face, as the horse bobs and spins 'round to the off-key honky tonk tunes, dries her tears as they trickle down her cheeks, a bittersweet release of joy and sorrow.

. . .

The following Monday, the summer coming to a close, Celia registers early for classes and runs into Sloan, hunched over the fall semester course catalog. He looks up at her, smiles, and says, "It's a conspiracy to keep me here—they close me out of required classes each year. They just filled Theories of Architecture. I'll graduate when I'm 52." He pushes the catalog aside, tucks a long lock of his blonde hair behind his ear and adds, "I saw your piece at last year's show." There's an awkward silence; Celia shifts her gaze to her shoes. "Oh, right, what I mean is, it was good, really good. No really, I mean it. That's why I brought it up."

She isn't sure why, but she opens up to him and says, "I've been completely dry all summer, my head in a book. I'm seriously terrified of starting up all over again."

"Definitely...know what you saying. Every September's a fearfest. I'm always thinking—will I totally screw up?" They laugh and chat some more and when they complete registration, he asks her to lunch, suggesting a Chinese place, a favorite haunt, a couple blocks north. "The food's pretty good—you know, family run."

Wind chimes jangle, when Sloan opens the door. They're ushered to a table and slide into a long red booth, the table covered with a thick, white cloth. Linen curtains are drawn against the blaring summer sun. The spacious room is cool, quiet, and dark. The waiter pours steaming green tea into two small white cups and places the silver teapot and a bowl of curled, inch-wide dried noodles on the cloth. The soothing sound of a trickling fountain near their table makes her feel relaxed.

Celia asks him about his summer. "I was off Cape Cod—on a boat—my uncle's," he replies. She notices that his forearms resting on the white cloth are browned, the muscles taut. "He's a fisherman and I helped him out, made a little bit of money I need for school." He tells her he was inspired to design a houseboat.

Sloan grew up in a happy, middle-class home, the only child of a second grade teacher and a longshoreman, in a two-bedroom clapboard house in Rhode Island. He was good with his hands, helping his dad with carpentry projects—a wood deck, a small, but ornate gazebo, and renovations like new kitchen cabinets. Surprisingly, she feels comfortable, almost completely at ease, around Sloan, as if she can tell him anything without being judged. She always picked at her food, unable to eat when out with someone new, but with Sloan, she is relaxed enough to enjoy her meal. She wonders why she isn't attracted to him. He is, after all, good-looking, his eyes kind and bright blue; his blond hair lightened by the summer sun—longer than last year and pulled back in a loose ponytail. She just isn't interested in Sloan Ford, she tells Theo, when he inquires about this new young man, her recently acquired acquaintance, for which he seems, in a fatherly way, proud. There is no attraction. That is all.

Part Four

Chapter Thirteen

DR. FLETCHER

ARRIVING WELL PAST DUSK and with the light of a nearly full moon, Leland derives some small comfort from beholding the impressive and stately Mill Valley Insane Asylum, without seeing the hand-forged iron letters welded to the high fieldstone wall announcing the facility's name and designation. Set among towering elms in a low, lush valley, the institution was erected around a central courtyard with two enormous wings jutting out diagonally, leading northeast and northwest, encompassing its 514 rooms. Leland is reminded of a photograph he saw in a book at school of an English castle. He'd never seen a building so big. With a tinge of excitement, he wonders about the other boys. Will they be nice? Maybe his father could stay with him until he settles in, he thinks, as the carriage bumps along the long dirt drive to the arched entry.

Could it be that no one is here? Leland wonders, as he and his father stand on the landing of a wide stair, dwarfed by the monstrous, wood double doors, the clanging of the bell unanswered on his father's second ringing, the black of the night threatening to engulf them. But the door suddenly creaks open a crack. An elderly man, the many carved lines in his face reminding Leland of a topography map, peers though. "And who have we here?" he asks, signaling a qualifier for admission. His teeth are gray where they aren't blackened, his eyes narrow as he focuses on Leland, who tries to stand still, but his right leg won't listen, bending at the knee, then kicking out in front of him in spasm, just missing the door.

"Leland Barrens…and I'm his father, Thomas Barrens. Dr. Fletcher is expecting us."

As father and son hesitantly step inside, Leland's gaze lifts up, drawn to the enormous dome above. A wrought iron chandelier hanging from a massive iron chain descends from the dome's center, barely illuminating the almost empty, circular stone room. Off to the side, a small wooden desk and Windsor chair stand alone. Tom lowers Leland's suitcase to the floor, gently, as not to make a noise in the hollow hall and dutifully follows the man to the desk. Leland stays behind. The man does not offer the seat to Tom, so Tom stands. After shuffling papers, the man retrieves a two-page document, hands it to Tom and directs, matter-of-factly, "Sign."

Tom tries to make sense of some of the sentences, rereading the ones that loop around and back again in double negatives. "In accordance with, but not omitting…and if relinquishing such action, notwithstanding…" When the old man clears his throat, ever so politely expressing his mounting impatience and hands him a long, black fountain pen, Tom dips it in the black ink and in jagged script, scratches his name. He hugs Leland tight, and then, without a word, walks out into the night.

When was the last time that Leland, now a boy of twelve, wet his drawers? He was five, and even that an unusual circumstance, when Warren Swift cornered him at the old school, threatening a beating with a gardening rake if he didn't hand over his new wool coat—burgundy with black buttons—and his cheese sandwich on pumpernickel, his lunch. Yet, as Leland follows behind the old man as he shuffles down a long, damp, dark hall, past dozens and dozens of closed doors, his hot urine lets loose, soaking through his drawers and trousers. This is especially troublesome, since he possesses no clean clothes, having been instructed to leave his suitcase behind in the front hall. "You sit that down right here," the old man had directed. When Leland hesitated to release the handle, the man inquired, with the respect he was accustomed to paying the boys at Mill Valley, "You hear me, you little scum?"

At the turn of the hall sit two men, side-by-side on a wooden bench, the fattest men Leland's ever seen, both bigger around than Mr. Henderson, the science teacher, who it was rumored by Leland's peers, got lodged in the water closet requiring the town fire chief to extract him—something to do with a crow bar and a fire hose. Both men rest their splayed-out feet on an old trunk set before them, their enormous bellies, twice as big as the biggest snowball Leland ever rolled, plopped atop their legs, reaching almost to their knees. The pant leg of the man on the right is hiked up revealing his fat ankle, which looks to Leland like the rotting trunk of a tree—dimpled, pock-marked and gray. Leland concludes that one of them said something funny, because they both let out a big guffaw, their jaws cocked back, snorting with glee.

"What's with your legs, boy? Can't keep 'em toppa yurz feets?"

"It's a disease, sir," Leland replies, hoping for, but sensing the futility in, eliciting sympathy.

"Ize thinks you had too much to drink." This sets them off again, their fat necks rolling back in waves, their hoarse laughter mixed with spit. "Room 492, Harry," the man on the right instructs, when he manages. Leland tries to hold his tears, but they pour down his cheeks. He mops his nose with his shirt sleeve.

Like the many doors they walk past, 492 has a large, square, wrought-iron lock above the knob, which Harry unlocks with a long, black key tied to a leather lasso extracted from his pants pocket. From the dim hall light, a triangular shaft cuts across the six-by-six foot room, barely illuminating a bale of straw in the right corner and a dented tin pot. When Leland hesitates at the open door, Harry places his hand on Leland's shoulder, which Leland assumes is a sympathetic gesture, but the old man shoves him in, slams the door, and turns the key. Aside from a narrow bar of light that falls beneath the base of the door, the room is black. Leland crawls into a ball, cold and wet, and sobs himself to sleep on the straw.

Leland rouses to a man gently shaking his shoulder. "Wake up, now. Rise and shine." His eyes nearly caked shut from dried snot and tears, Leland tries focusing on the man standing above him. He is tall, very tall, and thin, so thin Leland can see how the bones fit together beneath the pale, almost translucent skin of his face. His eyes are sunken, his nose is hooked and bent and he has no chin, or hardly a chin. Leland thinks he's never seen such an ugly man. He wears a long-sleeved white shirt, frayed at the cuffs, under a gray button-down vest. His gray pants, wrinkled and baggy, are gathered high in bunches at the waist by a worn, black leather belt.

"I'm Dr. Fletcher. Stand up, young man; let's take a look."

Leland's black hair is matted to his handsome face. He rubs his eyes with his fists and stands, his right knee buckling, then over-flexing straight, his left arm flying out and bouncing back like a ricochet. It seems to Leland that his body is programmed to betray him, to degrade him. Dr. Fletcher keenly senses the boy's mortification with the faulty mechanics of his flesh and revels in his disgrace.

"I said 'stand' not 'dance,'" a self-satisfied smirk slowly forming across the doctor's face. "Hmmm…we could put you to good use," he muses. "We could all use some entertainment here." Tapping his knee with his hand, he recites in up-tempo, "…one and a-two and a-three and a-four." Then, lets out a laugh.

"It's an illness, sir," says Leland, his head hanging low. "My father said you could help me, sir."

"Hmmm…tell me again—those last three words."

"Help me, sir."

"Now, tell me again, but this time, like you *mean* it."

"Help me, sir," says Leland, louder, but not more earnestly.

The doctor raises his voice to a shout: "Pathetic is what I call that. Is that all your good daddy taught you? Have you never begged God for help? How do you beg God, Leland Barrens? You get down on your knees, Leland Barrens."

Leland drops. An animal-like cry sounds from the deepest part of him and then, a desperate pleading, "Help me, sir. Help me, sir."

Dr. Fletcher steps closer and watches the boy beg and sob. He reaches down, places his large palm and long, bony fingers atop Leland's head, then strokes his hair and mutters, "Yes, my boy. Yes."

Chapter Fourteen

THE TREATMENT

IT IS AN ELEGANT WEDDING, 66 guests in attendance, although Leland is not among them. In hushed tones, it is said, "Dora looks ravishing," wearing an embroidered silk gown off the shoulder, and, "George never looked so handsome," wearing tails of the finest silk and a black satin top hat. Frannie did most of the cooking, arranging a spread of braised veal, candied ham, and chicken fricassee with braided breads and whipped sweet potatoes, on a green pleated taffeta cloth interwoven with golden thread. Five days following the celebration, when Dora is honeymooning in Italy, while her new home outside Philadelphia is being painted and readied by servants and Leland is three months now at "the hospital," as the family refers to it, Frannie comes down with pneumonia. Before her infirm state, Tom had inquired about the family visiting their boy, but was advised by Dr. Fletcher in a formal letter, to "let the treatment run its course without the emotional upheaval that a family visit might engender."

At any other time in her youth and middle age, Frannie's stalwart body would have fought the accumulation of fluid in her lungs, but her broken heart and spirit weaken her will. For now she is alone, her children gone, her nest empty, her husband hated for the loss of her family. She blames it all on Tom. The guilt she feels for sending Leland away is wholly suppressed. When her fever spikes to a dangerous level in the night and in her delirium she calls out for her only son, not her daughter, not her husband, muttering something incoherent about spiders and graveyards and a spoiling Sunday dinner left out in the sun, Tom ices her feet and lays a cold cloth on her forehead, but she passes the next morning, alone, as her husband sets out to fetch the doctor.

It is several days before Dora can be found and notified in Rome. The newlyweds arrive home too late for the funeral. Tom takes to drink, is soon fired from his job, and squanders the family's meager savings, tucked tight in a small, silk purse in the back of a kitchen drawer filled with knives and serving spoons. He is forced to let go the home. Too humiliated to impose on his daughter, although she has reluctantly offered her house, too proud to fall in front of George, he moves to a boarding house in an obscure village to the north. Dora will confide in no one that she feels whisked to safety on shore, before the family ship is engulfed by storm. Busy with fittings for new clothes and decorating her stately house, she fully gives herself to the role of doting wife, is happily with child by early spring, and closes the door, so to speak, on her own bad blood. She sends a letter to the hospital inquiring about her brother and receives word that he is "in good hands and showing small, but welcome, signs of improvement," bidding her and her husband "a touchingly warm congratulations on their marriage."

. . .

Leland is provided a uniform, fed a meager diet in a large, strictly silent dining hall, and left alone, locked in his room, where it is cold. He fears most the sound of keys jangling, the fiddling with the lock, Dr. Fletcher looming large at the door "paying a visit," demanding Leland take off his clothes, "a routine examination." The good doctor orders him on his hands and knees, then enters him from behind while Leland cries. If he tells anyone, Fletcher threatens, he'll never go home. That home, as if a mirage, is now gone.

Part Five

Chapter Fifteen

DESCENT

A WEEK BEFORE CHRISTMAS, Celia's mother calls to say she's planned "a little visit to New York." She'll be staying at the Stanhope for the holiday with Walter. A new one, Celia notes. They'll fly in, the long train ride too much for her back, which she recently pulled, she tells Celia over the phone. She complains she is no longer young, warning Celia to never do it, to never grow old. Then an unexpected sound...a little flutter of a forced laugh, like a frantic bird, coming from her mother. Celia is puzzled. She's never heard her mother attempt a joke.

A driver in a long black car deposits Cynthia at Celia's front door at 5:30, as the sun sinks down. She was expected to arrive "sometime after lunch." Walter is, "having a drink with a business associate." Due to dread, Celia has hardly slept.

There she stands, when Celia opens the front door, in a long, gray leather coat lined with gray fox, belted tight at the waist. Atop her head, sits a matching hat—also gray leather, lined in fur—its undulating brim angled, masking half her face. Her lipstick is frosted—a pale pink, almost white.

Her hair is longer than Celia remembers and neatly curled under at the ends, pointed to her chin. Celia accesses that her mother has taken on a new look. A large, crisp shopping bag from Bonwit Teller is dangling from her left hand.

She enters rambling about the weather and her trip: "They said 'unseasonably warm,' but it feels cold. I should have worn pants. What was I thinking? Wool pants. My ankles are cold in these stockings and my feet are sore. Something was wrong with the burglar alarm and they had to come fix it—almost missed the plane. The airport was too crowded. Maybe we should have taken the train. Who could sit for four hours like that, even with a trip to the club car? What I could use is a drink. Your place looks nice. Are you scared at night? I wouldn't want to live here alone. You can do it, I suppose. You're young. How's school?" It was the first time she asked.

Celia says, "good."

Her mother keeps on, without a pause. "Walter will probably meet us for dinner. He'll call. I gave him your number. Is the phone working?"

"Yes, Mom, the phone works. Do you want some tea or something to warm up? I bought some wine. Do you want a glass of wine?" Celia heads for the kitchen. Her mother follows behind, her high heels clicking on the floor.

Her mother takes the bottle of red from Celia's hand. "This is what you drink? I need to get you some decent wine. Oh, this will do. Just a little— pour me half a glass." Celia knows her mother will have two full glasses and that will mellow her. A little drunk is always a lot better when it comes to her mother. Celia purchased some cheese, grapes and crackers and puts them on a plate. "Don't eat it. It'll ruin your dinner," her mother warns. "Walter wants to take us to a place his brother-in-law went to. Sarintino's or something, in Soho. Have you heard of it? I don't want pasta. I don't know if their veal is any good. I gained weight. Only a few pounds, but with the holidays coming up, I don't want to get fat fat." Celia's heard this before, there's "fat," and that's bad, but "fat, fat," is dreaded. Her mother removes her coat and hat and smears on fresh lipstick with the aid of a small rectangular mirror she extracts from her purse. "Audrey Aaronson is getting a face lift. She's flying to the Caribbean. It's a guy all the Hollywood people are using. Maybe 42 isn't too young. I just wouldn't want him to pull it too tight. It should look natural. If I do it, I want it to look natural."

The phone rings. It's Walter. He'll meet them at the restaurant at 7:00. Walter, Celia learns, owned textile manufacturing plants in several countries and is "mostly retired." He is now a consultant, his job description so vague, Celia amusingly imagines he's undercover for the CIA. He has on one of those loud sweaters made from a patchwork of patterned fabrics like Bill Cosby wears. His hair is longish and shagged and dyed a one-color brown. His face is overly tanned—almost orangey. His beard and mustache are narrowly trimmed. He looks like the devil.

He is false and impatient with Celia. This is a chore, taking the kid out for dinner. He wants to get it over with. In this way, he is Celia's ally. When the waiter puts the check on the table, all declining dessert, Walter practically tackles the guy, pushing a wad of twenties in his hand to hasten dinner's end. The driver drops Celia off and she waves at her doorstep before their sleek black car speeds up Fifth Avenue to The Stanhope. Maybe I'm just overtired, she thinks, as she sits on the edge of her bed, tears welling, then spilling.

The following morning, Cynthia and Walter take the car to a bed and breakfast along the Hudson for a week and call when back to the city with news they were married by a pastor and that this remaining New York rendezvous is now, delightfully, their honeymoon. "Congratulations," says Celia, and hangs up. She realizes she doesn't know his last name and, thereafter, calls him Walter Who.

...

It isn't exactly clear to Celia why she starts to fall apart. School's going well—her teachers give her A's and often admire her work. Theo offers regular support. She even goes out these days, mostly with Sloan—to a movie or museum or tea house around the corner from school. It's the can't-get-out-of-bed blues, as if something essential is missing that allows her mind and body to work. It's a fast descent, as if one day, she looks around and nothing matters. *Why go on?* takes root. Theo prescribes an antidepressant, a last resort. Not a fan of medication, he believes change occurs from digging up the dirt. What he doesn't know is Celia's childhood secret, buried deep in the dark, moist earth. The drugs don't work. A new medication is prescribed.

Shaving off the edges of her life, she narrows things down to the essential to avoid flunking school. Her grades slip. Her focus and motivation dissolve. Enviously, she watches other students, even strangers on the street, energetically going about their lives, seemingly encompassed by a clear goal that encourages and propels their movements. What she embraced about New York has disappeared. Poof. It's now dog-eat-dog, dirty, bleak and cold, the appeal hidden behind a veil. The colors are bleached out; the buses screech and spit fumes; the gutters are littered with brown glass and condoms; greedy people intercept and steal her flagged cabs. She hates it. She hates New York. The crowds frighten her. There seems no boundary, none at all, between her and the world, as if the very space she inhabits is suddenly gone. Finally home, her emotions sink and settle underground, where they can no longer be found. To feel, to feel anything, she finds herself pricking her finger with a pin or burning her hand in scalding water readied for tea. A general consensus takes shape: she is a failure, a fake, a bore, a slut, stupid, ugly, and spoiled.

Except for Sloan, and of course, Theo, no one knows what she's going through. Theo had encouraged her to be honest with Sloan and she had told him the truth. He shared that his aunt, his mother's sister, suffered dark spells all her life. He said he understood and would be there for her in any way he could. But, Sloan's consoling messages on her answering machine go unreturned. Except for an inquiry from Dr. Applegate, wondering if anything is wrong, which Celia skirts, she hides from the world.

With no appetite, she gets broomstick skinny. The kind of skinny even sweaters and jeans don't mask. Nothing happens except side effects by taking the second antidepressant. Theo has this habit of covering his mouth behind his hand to hide his expression during their sessions and he often does this now, but Celia can tell he's concerned. Brushing off his prompts and questions, she mostly sits silently during her appointment, ten or fifteen minutes ticking by, when all she manages is, "Shit...I'm coming apart," her head bent down, picking at her cuticles. And in this way, as winter comes to a close and the warm afternoons hint at the first signs of spring, she becomes fed up with Theo and Freud and the fifty-minute hour, and everything else for that matter.

. . .

The note is penned across the top of her incoherent essay on Modrian: *Celia, come see me.* After class, Celia thinks she might somehow ignore Dr. Applegate's request, but the teacher brushes by her desk and requests, "Hey, do you have a minute? Hang around." Celia reluctantly sits back down, as the remaining students, jabbering and laughing about a party they attended, file out the door. Dr. Applegate sits down at the desk in front of Celia's and swivels around. "OK—something's up. I read your paper last night—it's just not anywhere near your usual work. Would it help to talk?"

She admires Dr. Applegate, only wants her approval. Anything seems doable but telling her how much she's struggling. Celia feels guilty about having everything and feeling she has nothing. And then the welling up. It's uncontrollable. The tears rise up, spill out, as hard as she tries to hold onto them.

"I just don't think I can talk about it."

"Sometimes, just tears are best. Let them come. It's OK. I can't tell you how many times I cried at your age. I don't care how adept you are— growing up can really suck."

Celia lifts her head to see Dr. Applegate's expression. She wears a warm, compassionate smile that seems to say, everything's going to be OK. I know how bad you're feeling.

"I saw your paintings in the studio—you've got a thin skin. Everything gets through. It'll help make you a good artist, but it's tough to go through life like that with that kind sensitivity to all the stuff that's thrown you."

Suddenly, Celia feels safe with Dr. Applegate. She felt this with Theo, too, but the awful truth was the clock was always ticking, the bills were always due him, and more than anything, she wanted a mother's love.

"Sometimes what we need is a change of scenery. Each year I recommend two students to two spring break programs. One's in Chicago; the other's in Arizona. Trust me, you want the Arizona spot. It's a painting fellowship for a week. You set up your easel outside, paint the desert, the sky—a plein air program. Let me know if you might be interested."

An escape, Celia thinks. She knows on the spot that she'd like to go. "Yes, thanks, really, I think I'd like to go. Thank you for thinking of me." Celia can't help it, even if it's inappropriate—she stands up and hugs her.

"Oh, wonderful, just wonderful," Dr. Applegate exclaims, hugging Celia earnestly.

Chapter Sixteen

OPEN SKIES

ARIZONA SEEMS LIKE A DIFFERENT PLANET to Celia, who pictures walking around in a spaceman's helmet, as if breathing the air requires special apparatus. The terrain, rocky and dry, looks like the lunar surface in images sent back from a moon shuttle. And it's hot—almost ninety degrees. A late winter snowstorm in New York had left the sidewalks covered in unsuspecting patches of ice. Twice, she fell flat on her butt.

It's the sky that takes her heart, azure blue with puffy white clouds, like cotton tails. On this backdrop, splendid mountains form a jagged horizon line, like a cliché snapshot on a corny picture postcard, but it's all true, right there in front of her. And there are critters. Who needs the zoo? In a desert wash, behind the motel, she sees coyotes, javelinas, chipmunks, a quail family, and other birds: red crowned cardinals and a tiny, long-beaked hummingbird, wings beating like wild, sucking in nectar from a bright yellow flower. And gnarly cacti, too, each one like a cartoon character stoically enduring the blazing sun. There are even tumbling tumbleweeds, just like in the song. The vibrant colors, compared to the washed-out winter hues of New York, give orders to the sluggish synapses in her troubled mind to fire. On her back, on the small deck off her room, the warmth of the wood radiating through her neck and shoulders, Celia views the clouds between the branches of Palo Verde trees and takes a deep breath that seems to fill her soul.

Her roommate, Leesa Jorgenson—a gangly girl, originally from Idaho, arrives late that night, her plane delayed from California. She has long, straggly brown hair and wears a wrinkled, boxy white linen dress to her knees and a long string of silver beads. After a brief introduction, Leesa immediately heads for the deck, "to de-stress." Celia watches her sit cross-legged, her back straight, breathing deeply, her hands resting palms up, her forefingers and thumbs pressed together.

After their days painting side-by-side, easels under the sun, Leesa and Celia sit sleepily on the deck off their room, welcoming the cool breezes that arrive each night, and watching the stars. Leesa talks about "divine guidance" and "astral energies," and describes her paintings as fluid abstractions that are "channeled." Celia doesn't know what to think of this New Age stuff. It intrigues her, but she's skeptical. As Leesa explains mantras, chakras, and varied meditation techniques, varied words pop into Celia's head like hooey and phooey and bunk and baloney. But, as the days progress, and Celia accesses that her roommate possesses an undeniable equanimity, she thinks there just might be something to this. It would be an enormous relief to know there's more than what's apparent during the suffering she sometimes feels. If, somehow, there is a "higher plan" and a "higher purpose," as Leesa describes it, Celia wants to know about it.

At week's end, the girls exchange phone numbers and promise to keep in touch. Celia is reluctant to return to New York, wondering if her outlook will remain bright. Once back, she heads to Barnes and Noble to buy books that Leesa recommended. One outlines how to start a meditation practice and Celia purchases all the paraphernalia for this: a silk seat cushion, a candle, incense (she chooses sandalwood), and a special incense holder. She adds her own touch—a bud vase with a pink rose. This is her little altar. She arranges it in the corner of her bedroom. There it is. It sits unattended for three months. There are valid excuses. She is very, very busy with school. Then, an odd thing happens, a kind of kick in the butt. She's standing at the bus stop, her head buried in a book, pretending not to eavesdrop, when she overhears a woman bickering about an ex-boyfriend, or maybe an ex-husband. "Oh, right. Mr. Spiritual. He walked around in this kimono and we had to redecorate the bedroom…some Eastern bullshit with Buddha statues and sandalwood incense. It was all show." It was the part specifying sandalwood that seemed uncanny, that made Celia think the message was for her. That night, she sits down on her purple silk cushion, lights her candle and incense, and follows the directions in her meditation book. Things don't go exactly according to plan. The idea is to focus on the candle to still the mind. *Think only of the candle,* the book instructed. *If your mind wanders, watch your thoughts; gently bring your mind back to the flame.* Ten minutes go by before Celia catches hold of her frantic thoughts which devise another strategy for fixing the running toilet, create a bizarre narrative for the guy she sat next to on the plane back from New York, ponder if the milk is spoiled, obsess about her upcoming final in 2D Design, and the zits on her chin. She concludes she'll never, ever, be able to do this.

Seated in prayer, a baby white unicorn curled at her feet, its muzzle resting on her lap, Lady Kamara tries reaching her faraway daughter to give guidance and assurance. Her heart fills with hope. Rejoice! Her daughter is seeking a higher plane. If only Celia would quiet her mind for even moments at a time, Lady Kamara could communicate, via the astral grid of light, and send a message of love and support. Yet, her plans are dashed. She will have to wait. Picking juniper berries, one by one, she feeds them to the small filly at her feet, who lifts her head and bats her long, white lashes in gratitude.

Chapter Seventeen

WHEN YOU LEAST EXPECT IT

GETTING AN INVITATION TO ATTEND Dr. Applegate's end-of-the-year party is a kind of coup around school and while Celia is flattered and accepts, she doesn't feel much like going. What would it be like, she wonders, to be herself at a party. She always feels she has to be "on," to smile, to ask appropriate questions, to come up with interesting responses to what she considers forced dialog. But Celia's overriding concern is: *Will The Wolf be there?* She's avoided him the past year and is not enrolled in any of his classes. Maybe she should ask Sloan to accompany her, but no, she isn't sure he's invited and feels bad about pulling back from him. She didn't rekindle their friendship when she started feeling better.

Celia can hear the laughter and music all the way down the hall. Dr. Applegate lives on the Upper West Side, near the Museum of Natural History, where her husband works. Their spacious apartment has a fireplace, elegant wood paneling and parquet flooring in the living room. Where there aren't bookcases, handmade contemporary quilts and folk art paintings line the pale green walls. The sofas are caramel-colored leather—

sleek and low—scattered with patterned pillows. Friends of her husband's are jazz musicians and a trio plays standards. Champagne is served by high school girls in black skirts and white T-shirts, who also balance silver trays of hors d'oeurvres: Endive leaves with bleu cheese and walnut filling; buttered pumpernickel with dill and salmon; and avocado and crab sushi rolls. It's fun to see the fashion design students dressed in wonderfully outrageous getups. Celia wears a tapered, white, sleeveless silk blouse, vintage satin, red elbow-length gloves with tiny white pearls at the seams, a red velvet mini-skirt, and faux-leopard pumps. Soon after her arrival, Celia spots Sloan. He's leaning against the far wall talking to a girl Celia hasn't seen before. He smiles at something the girl says, then brushes her hair from her face and kisses her. She's tall, thin and beautiful and Celia feels horrible--absolutely horrible. Why hadn't she seen he was so adorable?

At that moment, Chelsea Weiss, a graduating senior like Sloan, trips on a rumple in the rug while carrying two glasses of champagne across the living room and splashes a full glass down Celia's shirt. "Oh my God, I am like soooo sorry," she exclaims, staring aghast at Celia's wet chest, her double-A padded bra now fully visible beneath her sheer blouse. The room goes dead silent, even the musicians falter, but then carry on. Celia looks immediately to Sloan, who offers a sympathetic look, but shakes his head ever so slightly side-to-side, as if to say, pity, you've never had much luck. His gorgeous girlfriend, of all the humiliations in the world, rushes over with a napkin to help mop her up. Dr. Applegate apologizes profusely and offers to lend Celia a shirt. Celia babbles an illogical excuse about having to get up early the next morning, maneuvers her way to the master bedroom and frantically searches for her jacket, buried at the bottom of the mound of outerwear on the bed. As she creeps out the front door, she spots The Wolf off the kitchen flirting with one of the young servers, a petite blond, who looks a bit like Celia.

. . .

That summer and into the school year, Celia paints to escape. Holing up in her studio, the hours stretch long—mealtimes come and go without eating, sleep escapes her. The paintings are good, her best yet. Her slow, meandering walks around her neighborhood become jogs circling

Washington Square Park. She progresses to three-mile runs several times a week by late fall. Pretzels and Pepsi are trashed for salads and sparkling water. Little by little, she begins to find ways to keep afloat—her work and her jogging foremost. She hears Theo's voice in her head: self-care. Intending to dodge the looping audio-tape of recrimination in her head, she reluctantly sits herself down on her purple silk cushion, her candle lit, her incense billowing, in her baggy nightshirt, but makes no progress. None. Her mind just won't shut up. Calculating every tiny nuance of every tiny event—this *has* happened, this *might* happen, this most certainly *will* happen—has been her number-one defense. She won't give it up. "Control freak," she mutters, under her breath.

At school year's end, she boards a plane for Arizona with her paint box, folding easel and a suitcase, landing in Phoenix for a two-week stay at Seven Palms Inn, north of the city, near the McDowell Mountains. She longs to paint the vast Arizona sky, the warm, vivid colors of the West again. She once heard someone say that you meet someone when you're not looking, when you least expect it.

Chapter Eighteen

CLAYTON CUTTER

CLAYTON CUTTER OFFERS CELIA A RIDE when he overhears her ask the front desk to call a cab. "I've rented a car. Let me give you a lift into town," he interjects. Celia turns to see a tall man, probably early thirties, oddly dressed for the laid-back locale and warm weather—in a suit. His brown hair, slightly graying at his temples, is cut short—quite conservatively. His tanned face is handsome. He seems misplaced, Celia thinks, his city clothes and formal demeanor a better fit in spiffy digs on Wall Street or Park Avenue. "I'm Clay—a pleasure to meet you. I've been staying here, on and off, for a few weeks now, on business. Trust me, you'll wait an hour. Rightway Taxi—they'll send Billy. He'll be late and overcharge you." He flashes a toothpaste ad smile. She could swear his teeth actually sparkle. Celia feels her knees buckle. Under most circumstances, she wouldn't accept a ride from someone she just met, but he certainly seems safe.

"Are you sure it's not out of your way?"

"No, not at all...headed to an appointment at the bank. Explains the formal attire," he says, stiffening his posture, straightening his suit jacket with an exaggerated gesture. "It'll be relief to get back into my shorts and take a dip in the pool." Celia pictures his tall, tanned, glistening body emerging from the water and feels the ground under her feet sway. The valet pulls his car to the curb—a sleek white sedan without a speck of dirt, blinding in the afternoon sun. He doesn't wait for her reply…just walks a few steps back and opens the car door for her. She slips inside. The radio is on low; the air conditioning is on high.

Clay tells her that he works for a real estate development company on Long Island, about two hours outside Manhattan. He shares that he's "on the road quite a bit, which is too much for my liking." Recently, the company has him managing "the final touches on a large housing complex slated to break ground in the fall. If all runs smoothly, I'll relocate to Arizona in October." Here, he slips on his aviator sunglasses, turns to her and smiles. He's so handsome, she feels nauseous. "Wish I could offer you a return trip, but this meeting's length is anybody's guess. Call the taxi with an hour's lead and you'll be good." He fishes for the taxi's card in his wallet and slips it into her hand. "Maybe you'd like to join me later for a drink at the pool. Oh, let's say seven. Hope to see ya." This guy is smoooooth.

Celia wears her black bikini with a gauzy white knee-length skirt and sips chilled papaya juice with crushed ice and lime. The icy liquid descends to her belly; the frosty cold goes straight to her head. She leans back in the lounge chair, crosses her ankles and lets out a barely audible sigh. The setting sun streaks the sky pink and orange. The wind picks up, rustling the leaves and rippling the water in the pool. Clay sits on the adjacent lounge chair in navy and white swim shorts and an open button down shirt. They talk for hours, past midnight. He's funny, smart, attentive, ambitious. Oh, dear Lord, he's perfect.

They'll meet for dinner tomorrow night. He knows a wonderful Mexican place. She can't sleep. Every tiny receptor in every whirling cell has flung arms wide open to Clay. What is this strange buzz? She dares think it: love.

Celia declines wine with the appetizers he's ordered. She already feels drunk and she wants to be alert. She eagerly listens to his story. He's divorced. Two years. No kids. Claire was his high school sweetheart. They married young. She worked in her mother's hair salon in Mineola; he went to Hofstra University for a business degree and then, began the grind, the nine-to-five, working his way to project manager in a growing real estate firm. All Claire wanted was kids, but twice miscarried. Now, he's thankful. He began to see they just weren't right together and then, listed her faults for Celia to consider. Under the pale pink tablecloth, Celia crosses her fingers and prays she exhibits none of Claire's loser traits. "We just didn't want the same things...she was happy working at Isabella's, doing hair and nails. Weekends at Long Beach was all she wanted." He takes a small sip of wine and continues. "She hated planes—I wanted to travel. How can I explain it? Everything was rote—Friday nights meant chicken parmesan, Sunday nights meant barbecue. Mondays she volunteered at church. She didn't want to try anything new. I bought her a couple of dresses; couldn't get her out of her Lee's and flip flops." He shifts in his seat, then leans back, crosses his arms. "Losing the second baby was pretty tough. I told her to take her mind off things, maybe take a class, but all she did was sulk." Celia feels sympathy for Claire, but also wonders if her own attributes might measure up for Clay's approval. Yet, she foolishly misses the point. Clay Cutter is intent on moving up. Celia is unaware of her shining prerequisite: she comes from money. Clay now steers to this like a shark to blood.

Celia's evenings take on a surreal quality, as if reenacting one of those dreamy get-away TV commercials: flirtatious romps in the pool, candlelit dinners on restaurant patios, kissing under the stars. He takes things slow, courting her. "Wooed" is the operative word. Little by little, Celia reveals her family story, which includes, to Clay's delight, certain happy nouns like trust fund and Manhattan brownstone. Clay speaks little of his past. He doesn't tell her, for instance, that his father had just been promoted to factory foreman when he passed of a heart attack. Clay was eleven. His mother moved the family—Clay and his younger sister—to Mineola, where her family was from, using the life insurance check for a down payment on a small house, soon shared with Clay's grandmother and invalid aunt. Most of the income for the house and its five residents came from Clay's mother's Hillside Motor Lodge job—cleaning rooms during the week and working the front desk on Tuesday and Thursday nights. Clay worked the paper route, raked leaves from lawns and arranged scholarship monies and loans for his ticket out—college.

Celia does not learn that, at eighteen, he moved in with Claire into the basement apartment of her mother's house, where Claire ironed his shirts, scrubbed the floors, shopped for food, cooked his favorite meals, packed his lunch and, in between, gave perfect facials and pedicures to the coifed patrons of Isabella's. When Clay finished college, they married. Starting with his first paycheck, they put 30% toward their first home. She lay awake at night, decorating the nursery in this imaginary "picket fence" abode. When Clay got his second promotion, he promptly filed for divorce.

. . .

Standing behind Celia, Clay lifts her hair and runs his tongue along the back of her neck. She feels a tingle all the way down to her toes. He turns her to face him, cradles the small of her back in his palm, bends her back, and kisses her, hard. She thinks *Rhett Butler*. She feels faint. She is special, he whispers, in her ear. She is "the one." With the deft flick of his forefinger, her bathing suit straps slip off her slender, tanned shoulders. He kisses her along her collar bone, his tongue descending down to her small, pert breasts. Laying her back on the bed, he kisses her waist, then her hip bones, first the left, then the right, then tucks his warm hand under her bathing suit bottom. Celia holds her breath, but he releases her and sits up on the bed. "I want this to be right. Maybe it's old-fashioned, but let's wait. Wait 'til we're married. Celia, will you marry me?" She knows him twelve days. She says yes, even though a voice somewhere in her head, is saying no. *It is Lady Kamara, yelling as loud as she can, her advice unheeded.*

Celia deserves a big, beautiful wedding, Clay insists, a grand celebration of their eternal love, as they tally up the guest list. There are his "folks from the firm," 46, not counting their wives or significant others. His family list is small, however, just four—his mother, his sister and brother-in-law, and his mother's sister, Aunt Ellen. It would be fun to invite Kip Dempsey, Lloyd Packson and Denny Wexler from the golf club, too—he's taking lessons in anticipation of courting clients on the green. Celia will move to Arizona when she finishes school in June. They'll look for a house. He's certain he wants a family—at least two kids. When she doesn't feel dizzy, she feels numb. She thinks about calling Theo, telling him about her plans, but she knows he'll say slow down. She fears that losing momentum would mean losing Clay. She plows ahead, breakneck speed. Normal. That's what she'll be. At long last. Even if she didn't grow up in a normal household, she concludes, it won't stop her from creating a loving and stable home of her very own.

In a tizzy of wedding arrangements, Cynthia signs checks for the wedding, in addition to helping the young couple with a small down payment on a new home. Walter Who has a cousin at The Plaza, and even with relatively short notice—for the ballroom is often booked two years in advance—he snags a sought-after date: June 10th. Cynthia has her face lifted for the event and wears a pale yellow chiffon floor-length Chanel with a choker of pearls. She insists on a make-up artist for mother and daughter before the ceremony. Celia isn't used to the thick base of cream, powder and rouge, the eyeliner and globby mascara. She feels like a clown. It will be the first of her days wearing a mask in her new role. Her off-white gown is fitted through the bodice, low in the back, beaded in tiny pearls, and flounces into flowing silk. She wears a beaded comb with a simple, short veil. When Clay lifts the lace and kisses her, she's certain she's playing a part on a TV soap. She imagines the director hollering, "Cut—that's a wrap." She'll march off the set, slip out of her costume, back into her jeans, taxi home, and get into bed.

They honeymoon in Hawaii, Clay's choice. He booked a suite on the top floor of the towering Gerard Hotel, but they spend their first night as husband and wife at the honeymoon suite at The Plaza, before boarding an early morning flight. Crystal vases of white lilies adorn the bedside tables, flanking a quilted, emerald green satin headboard and a yellow satin bedspread. A crystal chandelier glimmers low. The curtains, yellow and white striped silk, are trimmed with emerald green sashes and fringed tassels. The city streets, nine floors below, are quiet save distant honking horns. Champagne is chilling in a silver bucket under ice. Clay unzips her gown. It falls to the floor and puddles at her feet. She's dreamt of this night for eleven months, for Clay insisted on waiting. All the doubts and fears swirling in her head are put to rest by his eager hands, his passionate kisses, his deep, ecstatic thrusting. As she drifts off to sleep, her head cradled in the soft satin-cased pillow, she thinks she must be dreaming, but she glimpses Clay reflected in the ornate gold-rimmed mirror by the window. He poses, smiles and winks at himself, his chest flared, his hands dug deep in the pockets of the white terry bathrobe with the gold-embroidered Plaza insignia.

. . .

Celia misses her period the following month. The baby's due mid-March. Every morning, for two-and-a-half months, she throws up. Trailing their real estate agent, Dottie Bendel, who shows the newlyweds the newly remodeled kitchen, the cathedral ceiling living room, and the four bedrooms in what will be their new home—a ranch with a view of the desert, a backyard pool and a swanky, built-in wrap-around barbecue— Celia politely excuses herself and christens the master bath by barfing up breakfast into the Kohler toilet.

Clay "unofficially" uses part of his construction crew from the site (a twelve-acre stretch of Scottsdale desert, where his company is erecting 40 condos with the cheapest materials possible hidden under stucco), to "touch up" their own home in the posh township of Paradise Valley, laying saltillo tile on the backyard patio and adding plantings to the front lawn. When the crew completes the outside work, Clay decides he wants the guest bathroom retiled and a skylight added to the living room. Celia will oversee the renovations, while awaiting the arrival of their little one.

Part Six

Chapter Nineteen

THE MASTER KEY

JUST SHY OF HIS FIFTEENTH BIRTHDAY, confined for two years, Leland awakens cured. *Is this a miracle?* he wonders, astonished, pacing his cell in small circles, his legs obeying his rule, no jerking out from under him, no twitching in his hips to jar his gait. He halts, holds his arms out straight, and lo and behold, steady. Tears of relief he weeps, tears of sorrow, for all he's endured. Dropping to his knees, he falls over and sobs in gratitude for his body born anew. Had it been that one time he offered his soul to God almost a year ago, bargaining with the Almighty to enact a cure? He'd considered prayer thereafter, but damned divine intervention, concluding that the red devil made the rules.

What he would learn months later fueled a rage as fierce as a cyclone. His physical ailments resulted from the aftermath of rheumatic fever, which he'd suffered weeks before his twitching began. His twitching, jerking movements, facial grimacing and mood changes mimicked, almost exactly, the symptoms of Huntington chorea, yet there was one marked difference. While Huntington chorea was incurable, the aftermath of rheumatic fever, called St. Vitus Dance, remitted on its own, within six months to two years. This remittance did not require treatment, its cause a certain type of streptococci, Lancefield Group A beta-hemolytic. His diagnosis by Dr. Arnold had been wrong.

Leland hides his recovery from the staff at Mill Valley Asylum, including Dr. Fletcher, as his plans of escape formulate. He reasons that if God offered a miraculous healing, he'll surely insure his safe passage to freedom. It is with this false confidence, with Dr. Fletcher kneeling behind him, banging into the boy harder and harder, faster and faster, that Leland grabs the bent handle of his tin bucket and with all the fury of a longstanding victim finally summoning power, hits the doctor fiercely and squarely on his head and knocks him unconscious. With Fletcher splayed on the floor, blood gushing from a deep gash to his head, Leland—his heart racing, his face red, his brow wet with sweat—pulls the ring of keys from Fletcher's pocket and flees with his bucket in hand to the small linens and cleaning closet two doors down—a closet he passed twice each day for almost two years now, on his way to the dining hall. He will hold vigil there until dark—just over an hour—and then, plain and simple, exit with his master key.

Part Seven

Chapter Twenty

INFIDELITY

IT IS IN CELIA'S EIGHTH MONTH of pregnancy that Clay begins the affair with Veronica, a real estate agent he met at the golf club. He can't say exactly why. It has something to do with Celia's growing size—her basketball belly, her swollen ankles, her fat feet that only fit into flip flops. But more than that, Clay perceives her now as a mother, not a lover. He compares what he has at home to what he finds around his job. A business woman is the perfect antidote to the same-old. Veronica is savvy and sophisticated in Clay's eyes. And just as luring, he can: Celia's stuck solid, with a child almost due. He likes the game—the deceit, the maneuvering from one woman to the next, all in the scope of an ordinary day. It spices things up. It doubles his receipt of adulation, his lifeblood.

Veronica Halsey is tall, lanky and brunette—opposite to the goods he has at his disposal. At 41, she's seven years older than Clay, but looks much younger by means of a personal trainer, a plastic surgeon, designer clothes and careful coifing. With an increasing share of her time required to maintain her youthful appearance, she relies on Clay's sexual interest to deny her advancing age. She's a knock-out who prefers married men; this is her fourth affair, if you count the one-night stand with the amateur baseball player in San Diego. She is married 16 years to an attorney specializing in real estate. Money comes to her in spades from her husband's seven-digit income and his lucrative investments in housing developments throughout the growing sprawl of suburban California communities. Clay especially likes slipping into the passenger seat of her black Mercedes Benz—inhaling the scent of her signature perfume (Yves St. Laurent's Opium), and new leather. When her husband travels, Clay has Veronica at home, atop the mink throw on the king size bed. More often, they meet at an empty house on the market, Veronica's bare back pressed against the kitchen's cool counter or the beige Berber carpet; and occasionally at the Hyatt, in a luxury casita near the property's edge, where celebrities and adulterers are discreetly assured by the resort's concierge of their seclusion and privacy.

After one such early afternoon rendezvous with Veronica, Clay takes the time to leisurely shower—to wash away the tangy odor of sex and semen—after receiving Celia's nervous and excited call that she's in labor and their neighbor, Janet, is taking her to Central Valley Healthcare. Dutifully, Clay hovers over his wife at the hospital, holding her hand, thinking of Veronica's long, tanned legs and diamond belly button ring, while Celia pushes and heaves, doing her Lamaze breathing. It's a girl. Clay chose Cosette. Celia thinks the name a bit affected, but goes along.

Clay likes the idea of a baby. It suits his image as a family man at chamber of commerce meetings, at sales conferences, and playing 18 holes at Copperwind Golf Club. Entertaining Clay's strategically chosen "friends," affiliated with work or the club, becomes Celia's domain. Two or three couples are invited to the house on weekends for small dinner parties, where Celia attempts interest and participation in conversations that run the gamut from where one has recently dined, golfed or vacationed to where one will dine, golf or vacation. Celia learns to cook elaborate gourmet dinners, for which she takes pride, but often feels she's running a catering business. She's worn out. Cosette is a poor sleeper and Celia is awakened three, sometimes four times a night. When Celia overhears the other moms at playgroup boast that Conner and Tiffany are sleeping through the night, she thinks she'll fall over from exhaustion and envy.

However, Clay is adamant that he wants a Martha Stewart wife, so Celia, on occasion, secretly picks up prepared dinners for her weekend dinner guests from a gourmet take-out place and, like a criminal hiding the evidence, shoves the plastic containers and waxed boxes—that contained the fragrant fried coconut shrimp, the succulent rack of lamb encrusted with something or other, and the delicately stuffed mushrooms—outside, into the bottom of the big, black garbage can.

During late night and early morning hours, while Celia nurses and rocks Cosette back to sleep in the nursery rocking chair, a lullaby tape on low, she reads books about childrearing to give her an edge. The love she has for her newborn child comes easily to her, but she knows she has not been privy to parenting skills, so she turns to research. She aims to raise Cosette so that the little girl might, she prays, grow up to possess a strong sense of self—something Celia is still fighting for.

With his growing presence in the community, Clay is offered a spot by Mike Varonti as Vice President of his reputable Arizona real estate firm. Although the increase in salary doesn't initially amount to much (for productivity will result in remuneration), Clay buys a Rolex, Armani suits and Ferragamo shoes at Neiman Marcus; books monthly facials and weekly manicures; and has a dozen shirts hand-tailored at Sergio's. Celia, on the other hand, looks overweight and worn-out. The baby weight won't budge.

It is largely the lack of sleep for over two years that plays havoc on her health, but factor in the undiscovered trauma that lurks beneath her interrupted nights and sleep-deprived days and the equation equals illness. Celia gets sick…low-grade fevers, fatigue, muscle aches. After tests and more tests, no doctor can figure it out. She's able to get through her days, but feels sick for over a year. Driving back home from Cosette's preschool (having turned three, she attends two mornings a week), Celia passes a new storefront that catches her eye: The Center for Integrative Healing. She pulls into the small parking lot. As she walks through the front door, Celia is unaware that she will begin, in earnest, the unfolding of a personal and spiritual journey that will wholly change her life.

Chapter Twenty-One

THE QUEST

D R. KERRIGAN HOLME, THE DIRECTOR at Center for Integrative Healing, is a petite woman in her mid-forties with closely cropped brown hair and hip eyeglasses, who has a PhD in psychology and practiced as a family therapist before turning her career on its head by becoming a hands-on-healer. She migrated west to find herself and start anew after her husband, the love of her life, died of cancer mismanaged by an oncologist at a top hospital in their hometown of Chicago. Fed up with all systems on which she thought she could rely, including traditional medicine and her own career offering traditional therapy, she explored and now employs a variety of alternative modes of healing, which she bestows upon her growing numbers of clients in her new, expanded office.

Dr. Holme's core belief—that energy medicine is the key modality to healing—assists her patients in reestablishing new energy patterns. "It's surprisingly simple," she explains to Celia, her large brown eyes gentle and clear behind her thick tortoise shell, rectangular frames. "You come in for an hour and recline on the massage table. I do a kind of light touch massage that helps me assess your condition and shift your energy. Most clients leave feeling peaceful and relaxed." Celia looks skeptical, so Dr. Holme tells her more. "When your energy is free flowing, you are in a state of health. When your energy is blocked, illness develops. In India, this energy is called prana. In China, it's called chi. You've probably heard of that. It's been the basis of healing modalities going back ages in history. This energy might be described as a luminous body that surrounds and mixes with the physical body. You've probably heard it called an aura." Glancing toward a diploma behind her, Dr. Holme continues. "I graduated from Barbara Brennan's School of Healing. She has schools all over the world. I went to the one in Florida and after four years, got a degree. They're known as one of the best places to learn hands-on-healing. Barbara Brennan's deeply rooted in the metaphysical, but also is a prominent scientist, formerly a NASA physicist. Hands-on-healing is used to cure diseases, help quicken recovery from surgery, for instance, or assist with emotional and spiritual healing." Celia is impressed, but still feels a bit nervous. Yet, she's exhausted resources available to her through conventional medicine. She's been sick for over a year now. In short, she's desperate.

During Celia's first appointment, some pretty strange stuff happens, stuff she wants to fully deny because it puts into question constructs she holds about herself and how the world around her works. Only several minutes into the session, she feels heavy, nearly leaden. This elicits a dreamlike state, in which she feels peaceful, more peaceful than she's ever felt. Then, something extraordinary…waves of blue light—the bluest blue washing over her. It starts at her head and moves down to her feet, then back up again, encircling her. It's undeniable, although she wants to think she's making it up. Kerrigan stands at the base of the table, her hands lightly placed atop Celia's feet, then works her way to Celia's calves, then thighs, then abdomen. With her hands hovering over Celia's lower abdomen, she begins speaking—softly—so that Celia strains to hear: "Here, we have a dark constriction," she says. "A dense blockage that I am lifting out. It's dissipating and now I'm flooding this area with white light." Kerrigan moves to Celia's heart, placing the tip of her forefinger in the center of Celia's chest, in the middle of her breast bone. "Your heart, dear one, has been hurt. You think you are not loved and this has caused you great pain, but you are loved by the masters of the celestial planes." Here, Celia starts to cry, progressing into sobbing. Her tears are so many that they puddle in her ears; she thinks to wipe her face, but her arms feel so heavy, she can't move them. She sobs for the pain she's endured and for her broken heart. Kerrigan sees Celia trying to contain herself and encourages her to let it flow. "It's a good release—clients often cry. Just let in come. It's all OK, more than OK. It's wonderful. Things need to come up and out." Moving behind Celia, Kerrigan places her fingers lightly atop Celia's forehead, standing like this for a long time. Celia isn't sure if she fell asleep, but the next thing she knows, Kerrigan is holding her hand, standing by her side, when Celia opens her eyes. Kerrigan warmly smiles and says, "We did good work today. There's nothing to do; just be with it. Let it integrate."

For the next hour, Celia goes about her day as if a different person. She needs to run an errand—buy a few groceries at the supermarket—but the experience is otherworldly. She marvels at the groupings of colorful fruits and vegetables, as she places apples, broccoli and blueberries in her cart, as if she's seeing them for the first time. Their colors are more vivid than she has ever experienced. Edible gifts from God—in reds and blues and greens—in different shapes and sizes, to nourish the body! She stands in awe. Life is nothing less than a miracle. It's as if she's on some kind of wonderful mind-altering drug. She gets an enormous kick out of the drawing of a cow on the milk carton and giggles aloud. Alarmed, the woman standing next to her, carefully perusing the cottage cheeses, quickly grabs a container and steps aside. Celia has purchased this milk for years and never noticed this adorable, whimsical cow. She's been living life in a trance, in a slumber, she thinks, and is suddenly awake, attuned to the most minute detail, the sheer wonder.

And then it stops. The awe leaves her, just like that, as she heads home, getting stuck in traffic behind construction, hearing depressing news on the car radio. She tries to hold onto it, but it disappears, goes up in smoke. That night, however, she sleeps deeply and restoratively, and feels more energetic for the next few days. That feeling, however fleeting, is the first time she can deem her state of mind happiness. This, she understands, is what she's always been seeking.

The following week, she eagerly returns for her next appointment. Kerrigan assures Celia that she'll get better and better, little by little, at holding the space of joy and tranquility induced by the sessions, for which Celia is so enamored. Celia visits weekly for two months and feels almost wholly better, physically. Her back and neck aches disappear; she has more energy. Her low-grade fevers diminish during these two months, until they vanish entirely. Her ability to hold her joyous states also improves. As the weeks unfold, Kerrigan introduces Celia to what will become Celia's main meditation practice—a series of guided meditations. Kerrigan encourages her to listen to the tapes regularly with the idea that Celia can learn to shift her energy herself, as well as practice prolonging her peaceful and happy states.

Celia is hesitant to reveal her new findings to Clay, who is skeptical when it comes to anything outside the box—particularly all things New Age. When Celia had suggested taking Cosette to an acupuncturist, for instance, for a minor bicycle accident for which she was slow to recover, Clay wouldn't hear of "taking her to a quack," adding, "Next thing I know, you'll be giving her snake oil." Even vitamins and herbs are discounted. Clay only trusts prescriptions from medical doctors. So, Celia hides her tapes; she hides her new spiritual practice. He seems so preoccupied anyway, with his new job, which requires late nights at the office, weekends wining and dining bankers and prospective clients or doing deals on the golf course—or so she thinks. Clay is continuing to carry on his affair with Veronica, who he sees twice, sometimes three times a week. His ability to manage the intricate schemes and lies is insured by his careful orchestration of the minutest detail, as if he's an accomplished criminal. He feels no remorse for his infidelities, indeed, he feels wholly entitled to the conquest of his sexual pursuits, even on occasion orchestrating a tryst on business trips to Dallas and New York, spicing things up beyond Celia and Veronica. He enjoys the deception as much as the sex. The power is the kick.

With more energy—her health fully restored—and more available time when Cosette begins full-day kindergarten, Celia applies herself to her appearance, losing the last of the "baby weight" with a rigorous jogging schedule, styling her hair, returning to wearing lipstick. Kerrigan helps her refine her diet and when Celia makes her fresh vegetables juices of parsley, celery and wheat grass, she thinks of The Wolf, his health foods and regimented diet. She wonders what he's up to these days, what he's painting. She's surprised to remember him fondly with the years now behind her. And moreover, she returns to her art making.

Setting up an art studio in the guest bedroom, she tackles her first canvas as if famished eating a gourmet meal. Wholly preoccupied with her new role as wife and mother, she forgot how much painting meant to her. What a relief it is to lay out her colors, to apply her brush to canvas, to see the colors come alive, to lose herself, once again, in her art. There's an assuredness in her style now—a fusion of practiced technique with a more mature approach gained by life experience. While Cosette's at school, Celia spends her days in her studio. Next to her easel, Celia strategically placed a child's easel with an attached pad of paper and on occasion, gets extra hours in during the afternoons and weekends, with Cosette smearing fingerpaints or scribbling with crayons. However, sharing art studio time requires a little more strategy, when Cosette gets fussy.

"Mine isn't as good as yours," Cosette says, plopping down on her bottom, crossing her legs, digging her elbows into her knees, her palms squishing her pouty face.

Celia places her brush on her palette, steps back and assesses Cosette's scribbles. "That's really not true, sweet. Mine looks contrived compared to yours, which is freer, more alive."

"What's contrived mean?"

"From the head, not the heart."

"But, I'm drawing with my hand."

"But, your hand is connected to your heart. And your shin bone's connected to your…" Celia starts singing the silly song and Cosette starts to laugh, jumps up and starts scribbling again, mother and daughter, lost in color, line and form, side by side.

As Cosette matures, so does her artistic skill and talent. Celia tapes her drawings and paintings throughout the house—in the dining room, den, kitchen and along the hallways. She marvels at the simplest things about her daughter, foremost, how she gets around. She skips everywhere, sashaying through the kitchen, back through the living room, out the patio door and around the backyard. How she spontaneously laughs—a deep, rich laugh from her belly. How she bursts into unrestrained tears, like the time her ice cream fell off the cone at Dairy Queen. The quality of so much authentic emotion, the exhilaration and the tears, is both thrilling and painful for Celia to witness. Celia gives Cosette the love she never had, yet that giving comes through a veil of grief for what Celia was denied. Celia mourns her lost childhood. She sees—not just in theory, but in practice—the meaning and impact of a mother's love. It hurts to see all the ways in which her own beginnings lacked, but it also fosters a deep compassion for her own struggles, encouraging forgiveness for her faults—her insistence on control, her over-worrying, her bad choices with men. She doesn't yet know how bad.

As Cosette progresses through elementary school with after-school sports, activities, and friends filling her afternoons, Celia relishes her uninterrupted days in her art studio. When her paintings begin piling up in stacks against the walls, she gathers the courage to bring photographs of her work and two choice paintings to a gallery she's had her eye on. It's a small gallery in Scottsdale that she feels resonates with her contemporary style. Most of the other galleries in the downtown district, famous for the tourist trade, sell paintings of cowboys and Indians, or a cactus silhouetted against a sunset. Lara Cordinger is the owner and although Celia is shaking from nerves, she greets her with a firm handshake and a show of confidence. Lara is enthusiastic about her work and wonders if she might come by Celia's studio to have a better look.

Lara visits the following week and agrees to represent her, beginning with the inclusion of two paintings in a group show and a solo exhibit to follow. Celia is ecstatic. She calls Clay to share the news, who promises to take her to dinner at Portobello, her favorite restaurant, to celebrate the following week, after he closes a deal that's pending. When these plans finally come to pass, months later, they morph into his usual networking schemes. Celia doesn't express her hurt, when he invites Josie and Chet Hammer to come along—Chet is "a good contact," he met at the club, who, not that it really matters, has a gummy smile and bad breath.

With Clay working late, after putting Cosette to bed, Celia often listens to one of the tapes that Kerrigan has suggested. This meditation practice is fun, a world apart from her previous attempts to plant herself down, still her mind, watch her thoughts. She recalls reading that there are many types of spiritual and meditation practices and that it sometimes takes time to find one you like. These tapes, Celia reads in the accompanying brochure, were made by Sanaya Roman and Duane Packer. Duane was a practicing scientist (after obtaining a PhD in geology), when he began seeing people's auras—fields of subtle, luminous colors surrounding a person or object. A classic skeptic, he was faced with contradictions between what he saw and what he believed. Sanaya helped him progress on his journey and they formed a partnership to help others on spiritual paths. The brochure explained that Sanaya channels a guide named Orin; Duane channels DaBen. Celia had heard of channeling, but wasn't sure what it meant. She thought of teenagers hovered over a Ouija board summoning the spirit of Elvis. The brochure said channeling was a form of communication with higher beings—like angels or ascended masters, or even your higher self. It's tuning into another frequency to get information and messages. She wondered if this could be true and then, considered that many of the world's religions were predicated on their founders communicating with God or angels.

There were varied tapes to choose from, each one thirty minutes. The tapes came in packs of eight and the instructions entailed progressing from one to the next. In the first few tapes, Celia followed different sounds that helped to align her energy. Each sound set a specific frequency and once that frequency was set, she followed the guided journeys. Some journeys took her to different astral planes, actually traveling a gridwork of light. Far above the earth, she interacted with angels and high beings. She tells no one about this for fear she'll be hauled straight away to the loony bin. As much as she tries to deny these visions and discourses, the experiences are as real to her as the tree outside her window or the shoes on her feet. Some of these beings are Hollywood-type angels, as in the movies…hazy outlines of white light in the shape of snow angels. Others are saints that she read about in books, who seem to still exist, just not on Earth. All have one thing in common, they emanate love. Love is the main frequency in these celestial realms. She's surprised to find that she's adept at reaching a euphoric state by doing these meditation tapes. She feels peaceful, as if she's floating, serene, blissful. The tapes' instructions point out that the guided journeys raise your vibration and enhance the light within your aura.

"Rejoice," exclaims Lord Myran, wearing his gold crown for the occasion, raising his goblet above the crystal table on the terrace of The Temple of Light, where his wife and the Council are seated, making a toast to their daughter for her recent achievements. Donning her finest silver robe and a coronet of diamonds and sapphires, Lady Kamara takes a sip of the sweet nectar. Two white peacocks with pink iridescent plumes stroll among a trio of angels serenading the celebrants with bejeweled bronze harps. The scents of myrrh and frankincense waft in the gentle breezes.

Celia's favorite tape is called "Age Regression," in which she's instructed to re-parent herself as a small child. On the first go around, she has an aversion to this "healing the inner child" stuff. It seems the very worst of the New Age rubbish. There are certain words and phrases that she abhors. "Inner child" is right up there with buzz words in the art rags she reads like "cerebral" and "cutting-edge." And for some reason, she feels almost queasy when she hears someone say "paradigm" or "synergy." But, she seems to tune into something significant with this tape, recreating a narrative that has her mother and father loving her.

She begins weekly yoga classes at a nearby yoga studio, also at Kerrigan's suggestion, and buys a few books there, too, one which she finds enthralling, about the life of Paramahansa Yogananda, learning that the revered Indian guru, following the guidance of a lineage of spiritual masters, brought the ancient practice of yoga from the East to the West. Celia is fascinated to find that when Yogananda died, in 1952, the mortuary reported the absence of any visual signs of decay of his body for months. When her doubt about her spiritual practice occasionally surfaces, this kind of scientific evidence lends validity to her new pursuits, making her feel less dubious. Three times through she reads the story of his life, which entails his spiritual journey, pausing to gaze at the black-and-white photographs of Yogananda on the cover and throughout the book. She sends away for a small portrait photograph of him, which she tucks in her wallet. From time to time, she reaches for it among her everyday chores—stopped at a red light in the car or discreetly in the grocery checkout line—beholding his face so gentle, his eyes so forgiving and kind. She likes to imagine that he's always with her.

. . .

During the winter months of that year, Celia spends much of her time preparing for her upcoming gallery show. The gallery is small, but she'll need to produce four more strong paintings to add to her stock. When the last of the paintings is complete, still drying on her easel just two days before the show's opening, Celia takes a long, hot bath and sends up a prayer for success.

While four paintings sell to varied collectors, eight canvases are purchased by one man, Edmund Orinston, who Lara describes as the top art collector in Arizona. His sprawling, contemporary Scottsdale home and penthouse apartment on New York's Upper East Side are filled with works of art. He invites Celia and Clay to his house to get to know his "new art star," he calls her.

Touring his 10,000-square-foot home—more museum than house—Celia's relieved to find that Ed Orinston has a good eye. His collection is varied and thoughtful and he likes to pick out and purchase what he calls "the artist's prize," meaning the best work of an artist's series, or the entire series, if he feels like it. He has, in Celia's estimation, chosen what she considers to be the best paintings of her show. He travels the world, going to galleries, museums, and art fairs, keeping abreast of emerging artists, and often flies to New York for Sotheby's and Christies sales to view and bid for artworks he says, "I just can't live without." His money, big money, comes from varied patents on industrial processes. He is part inventor, part entrepreneur.

Celia is thrilled to find he's hung her paintings in a wing he recently built, which includes a music room for his new hobby, playing the piano. He is one of the most likeable people she's met—humble, witty and smart.

Celia is surprised that Ed offers her and Clay a look at the works of art in the upstairs bedrooms, and when they climb the wide bleached oak stairs and enter the master, she's stunned. There, center stage, hanging over the side table is her!—the painting of her by The Wolf. She's dizzy and sick. She thinks she might throw up. "Oh, my," she manages to emit. Both Clay and Ed turn to her. "Oh, it's just that, um, I know that artist. Well, you see, he was a teacher of mine in art school—at SVA—at School of Visual Art, in New York. That's a Harlan Lee Wolfe." Saying his name makes her knees shake.

"Yes, indeed," exclaims Ed, who smiles wide with pride. "Well, well, small world." Celia is panicked, wondering if either Clay or Ed might see the resemblance, but her hair is long now, no bangs, and the painting is stylized, so Ed doesn't make the connection and Clay is blessedly distracted by the sweeping view out the floor-to-ceiling window. "He's making a comeback these days—have you heard?" asks Ed.

"Oh, well, no. I haven't actually, um, kept up."

"Paul Booth, his dealer, New York's *top* dealer, as you know, is giving him a one-man show next year. First show in almost thirty years, now that some realist artists are making a comeback." Celia nods, turns from the portrait and quite rudely walks straight out the bedroom as the two men follow, confused.

Chapter Twenty-Two

PEACE

AS WINTER TURNS INTO A DESERT SPRING—with the sweet fragrance of orange blossoms permeated the hot, dry air and bursts of flowers blooming everywhere, things start to get a little weird for Celia, as she makes progress with her spiritual practice. These "interactions," in her guided meditations, at first few and far between, become easier for her to access and she eagerly seeks these otherworldly chats with her "pals in high places," as she endearingly thinks of them: Paramahansa Yogananda and occasionally, his guru Sri Yukteswar. There are other saintly beings, too, who sometimes come in and out of focus, who she has yet to identify.

Lady Kamara yearns for Celia to reach her in the astral planes. She is so close. Sending her a glorious wave of light, its essence love, for now, she consoles herself, will have to suffice.

It is love, pure love, Celia finds in her meditations, not the deceitful intentions of Clay whose actions fuel his own aims, for she now clearly intuits his desiring a house, not a home, a lifestyle, not a life with her. Celia grows weary of reaching out to Clay, of giving her heart with no reciprocation. On the surface, anyone can see, and they often remark, that he's "quite the catch." Cosette's friends' mothers and the secretarial staff at Clay's office think he's a true charmer, so handsome, and oh, that smile! They see that he buys his wife expensive things…how can Celia find fault with a new diamond wedding band, a top-of-the-line SUV, and an account with Fleur de Lis to deliver two towering floral arrangements for the foyer and dining room every Saturday night when they entertain. But, that's the thing that she discovers; it's not for her, but to impress others.

When Clay intuits that she's onto his game, he pulls a card out of his sleeve like a deft magician's sleight of hand, appeasing her with a little dazzle until the next go around. Something small always suffices: a flattering remark about her appearance, a short phrase of recognition about her parenting, a compliment about dinner served. He tosses a crumb and she eats it like buttered toast. Otherwise terse, void of kind words, he intends to keep her on her toes. He uses the same tactics with his staff at work.

Part Eight

Chapter Twenty-Three

EDYTH

LELAND BARRENS FINDS HIS WAY to freedom without a glitch, walking up Valley Road, the sun rising in the glorious sky he's not treaded beneath in almost two years, due to his confinement. The towering Mill Valley Asylum is now a disappeared silhouette nine miles behind him, an expanse he's trekked in the quiet and black of night. Thumbing a ride from a carriage carrying produce to the next town over, he accesses a map at the post office and sets out to hitch home—to his mother and father, to his own bed, to his own room. This two-day journey, alternating long stretches on foot and various rides by generous drivers, many sporting their first cars—shiny, black Model T Fords, lands Leland directly in front of an unfamiliar building, his former home, now painted a dark gray, with an unknown table and four mismatched chairs on the small swatch of front lawn. Just by ringing the bell, he learns from the new resident of his mother's death, of his father's destitution, and of his own homelessness. "Reckon you want to be visiting your sister then," when Leland inquires about Dora's whereabouts. "Wish I knew where to tell you," the woman says before quickly shutting the door.

Dora's husband, George Rutherford, established the hub of his import and export business in Philadelphia, but Leland is without this critical knowledge. Their elegant home, just outside the city, with its seven wallpapered bedrooms, six fireplaces, and polished oak floors, and the bustling activities of their two children and four servants, is all but a mirage to the adolescent boy who has no money, no food, no place to call home, just the clothes on his back—a navy blue uniform. Busy with dress fittings, redecorating the parlor and sitting room, as well as luncheons with the ladies from the Sommersville Women's Club, Dora has put her estranged family almost entirely out of her head. Her infrequent letters addressed to Dr. Fletcher have been promptly and cordially answered, assuring her of sisterly empathy and Leland's good care.

Slipping beneath barb wire fences, picking pears and apples along the way on private farms, and stealing two loaves of bread from the back of a bakery truck, has kept Leland fed. As he dejectedly walks on, sleeping the previous night under a willow tree when his feet would carry him no further, his head hung low, his face gray with dirt, he passes a graveyard, where two men push their shovels into the hard soil and toss the dirt. He solemnly stands watching them, thinking of his mother beneath the ground, and weeps. He wipes his wet face with his sleeve and takes a deep breath, overwhelmed with fear, knowing he now must fend for himself.

"I'm looking for work," he yells out. The men lift their gaze to him, rest their blades on the earth, and wipe the sweat off their brows with their muscled forearms. The older of the two, the planes of his face sharp, his complexion dark, hollers back, "Talk to Fitz—down the road a piece." Leland walks on thinking he'll lie about his age. *Will this work?* he worries. He's grown tall and broad, like his father, although he's thin from lack of proper nutrition. Soon he'll turn fifteen, and he just might pass for sixteen because of his height. He's matured into a handsome young man, his shoulders wide, his jaw angular, already sprouting the beginnings of a beard. His straight black hair was shaved off twice a year in the asylum, but the "cut time," as they called it, was coming due just before his escape, so it's now long—hanging over his forehead, plastered on the back of his sweating neck, his soiled collar.

...

"I can start tomorrow," Leland says, his hands burrowed deep in his pockets, his chest flared, standing erect. Fitz, a fat man with a thick, unkempt graying beard, chewing gum, smacking his lips, studies him hard, says nothing. Nervous, Leland looks to the floor, but then lifts his chin and stares him straight in the eye.

Spitting his wad of gum in the waste basket, he tells Leland: "You says you're sixteen. Goddamned bullshit. Who ya kidding? You ain't strong enough for digging, but I need seeding, mowing and trimming. Be here at six—sharp. Day goes 'til four. Don't fuck with me, boy. Pay day is Friday. Now get."

After sleeping in the rear doorway of the old church for a week, Leland rents a room at a boarding house on Roredon Road. Hot showers, hot meals and a roof over his head—that's all he wants. Those first few months, he lives intent on and contented by meeting his basic needs. He relishes the simplicity of his new life—its insistence on survival. It prevents him from reviewing his misfortunes in the past. It prevents him from dreaming of a future.

It is at the boarding house that he learns (from the knowledge of a traveling doctor, who intently listens to Leland's story), of his misdiagnosis, of his unnecessary confinement. His rage impels him to smash the windows of the town's physician's office off Avery Avenue in the middle of that rainy Friday night, and drink himself sick for two days and two nights. When he returns to work on Monday, he's sobered up, but still seething. It is on this overcast October morning that he first sees Mrs. Edyth Bert visiting the grave of her departed, her husband of seven months, who died, along with his brother, she tells him, in a summer boating accident off Martha's Vineyard. She surely is not pretty, but not exactly ugly either, although her stubby legs and boxy frame, with no indentation for a waist, and no discernable neck, remind Leland of an icebox. *How old is she?* he wonders. *Not yet eighteen*, he assesses. The smooth skin of her hands, the vulnerability in her pouting expression, make her more a girl than a woman.

It begins drizzling as she softly speaks, asking Leland about a grave being dug next to her late husband's, extracting a black silk scarf from her purse, folding it neatly in half, placing it atop her head and gracefully tying it beneath her double chin. For a fleeting moment, Leland pictures pulling that black fabric tight until she gasps for breath. The vision makes him dizzy and he wipes his brow with the back of his hand, a gesture to rid the horrid thought from his head.

Before she snaps shut her purse, she pulls out two striped peppermints, offering one to Leland, who takes it from her open palm. This tiny touch, as his calloused fingers graze her flesh, makes her step back in surprise, her face flushed. In Edyth's eyes, Leland looks virile—his chiseled jaw and cheekbones browned from long days in the sun, his broad shoulders pulling a green jersey tight across his chest. She pictures placing her palm on the rough stubble of that bronzed cheek, wet from raindrops. Leland intuits an opportunity at this passing moment, an open window, even if just slightly ajar, and offers to walk her to her car. By the time she pulls away from the curb, he's scored an invitation to supper. As he heads back to work that morning, passing a double row of hedges he's just flattened and a cluster of headstones guarded by a sole stone angel on her pedestal, her dreamy face devoured by icy winters, he thinks of riding in that fancy car of Edyth's, of home cooked meals, of her soft, pale flesh and peppermint breath.

...

"I'm feeling a little tipsy, I guess," says Edyth, grasping the dining table's edge to regain her balance. "Maybe too much wine," she says, blushing, making her way to the kitchen to retrieve the coffee, already brewing. "Do you take yours with cream? Sugar?" she yells out to the table where Leland sits, not having enough experience or manners to bring the dirty dinner dishes to the sink, but appropriately dressed, wearing his new pants and crisp, button down shirt for the occasion. He's never had coffee. He yells back, "Sugar." With his alert eyes, he observes the signs of money—her inheritance from her brief marriage: the grandfather clock, which has already chimed twice on the hour since his arrival, the floral-patterned china from which he's eaten his succulent roast hen and stuffing, the cushioned chair on which he's seated, the tiny rosebuds on the wallpaper flickering in the candlelight. He's drunk from wine and pleasure.

After two pieces of blueberry pie, which Leland exclaims is the best he's ever tasted, they sit awkwardly on the sofa, Leland finally summoning enough gumption to take her hand and say, "I like you," as he brings his face close to hers. She closes her eyes and he kisses her lightly on the lips, qualifying as his first kiss. When he pulls back to assess her response, hoping he might kiss her once more, she bows her head to avoid his eyes, but does not retract. So, he tries again, this time feeling the pulse and heat in his groin.

Leland feels victorious, for he only expected one kiss that evening and he's had two. This gets him into a talkative mood and he rambles on, still holding her hand, about his childhood—altering and embellishing the story. He is an orphan, he tells her, and he omits the entire narrative about Mill Valley Asylum, which he wants to forget.

Edyth brings her white handkerchief, trimmed in lace, to the corner of her eye, when she tells Leland the story of her late husband, a widower himself, "a heavy-set man," she says, who was almost twice her age, and an accountant. "He was well-off and had a stock portfolio," she says, with pride. In actuality, Geoffrey Bert was categorically obese—over 400 pounds—and sexual relations with her husband felt to Edyth like trying to come up for air in a sea of flesh. He also was more than three times her age. On their day of betrothal, she was sixteen and he had just turned fifty-two. "Maybe the Almighty wanted them joined in heaven, he and his former wife…it does get you thinking," she continues, bringing the hanky to her cheek, although there are no tears. Edyth and her mother (who was a seamstress by trade, her father a stone mason), helped the widower with his washing, ironing, and cooking for a reasonable fee, when he was left all alone. Edyth sometimes stayed for dinner. "One thing led to another," she says of their courtship, lowering her gaze, batting her lashes. "There was no kin to help. His missus been barren."

When Leland departs that evening and steals one more kiss at her door, whispering, "You smell so good, like a field of flowers," nuzzling his nose in her neck, where she's sprayed her floral perfume, she invites him for dinner the following Friday, thinking what a gentleman he is for taking things slow, for his flattering remarks, for being a kind and patient listener. *He needs caretaking, that's for sure, and I'm good at that*, she assesses, humming to herself, washing the dinner and dessert dishes, wiping the countertop. In bed that night staring at the ceiling, the coverlet neatly folded at her chin, she frets about his age—just sixteen. She's older—just by one year, but still. And his line of work...is that acceptable? Yet, he's strong and capable, and like her father, he works well with his hands to make a living and she can't stop thinking about that sweet way he held her hand and complimented her perfume and her dinner. Slipping her fingers beneath her wrinkled cotton nightgown, she finds her aching, warm center and thinking of Leland's fine-looking face, his soft kisses, she rubs harder and faster, coming in waves of pleasure, then soundly sleeps.

...

That following Friday night, before she's even put her lemon meringue pie on the pressed tablecloth, Leland reaches across the table and kisses her—this time long and hard—his eager tongue exploring her mouth. A fork falls to the carpet and flustered, she stands up to retrieve it, but he meets her, crouched on the carpet. When they stand, he embraces her, breathes in her rose and lilac scent, his warm breath on her neck. She unbuttons the pearl button at the top of her blouse, revealing the rounding of her full breasts. "You are the most beautiful thing in the whole wide world," Leland whispers, hesitating to touch her, to put the tip of his finger on that miraculous ivory flesh. Then, he strokes her, ever so gently, his forefinger running over the edges of her blouse, grazing her breast. He looks up to her face then, but her eyes are closed, her head is back. He can't help it, bringing his lips there to the deep crease, finding her white bra, unbuttoning the remaining three buttons of her blouse, cupping her in that stiff white lace in both of his hands.

Then, he releases her. This is more than he dared to even imagine. She'll think he's dirty if he wants more. And in this way, Leland teases her for months, each visit daring to go a little further, until she is overwhelmed with desire.

When he appears at her front door, uninvited, that Saturday morning—two months after they meet, following a dinner the previous evening, Edyth still in her nightgown, her hair uncombed, the morning tea not yet brewed, she knows he's come to have her. When he releases, deep inside her core, panting, his face flushed and contorted, he falls atop her breasts and pleads, "Marry me, marry me, please. I love you."

. . .

Benjamin Barrens is born on the bitter cold, but luminous morning of New Year's Day, 1931, which Edyth hopes is a sign of new beginnings, as Leland took to drink soon after their wedding. Their arguments, lately, revolve around money. Edyth doesn't want to give up the house, but they're already four months past due on the mortgage and the bank has threatened foreclosure. Her stock portfolio has lost 80% of its value and even taking in a boarder, they struggle to make ends meet. It's rumored that Roosevelt, aiming to halt further economic ruin, will announce the close of all financial institutions, intent on stopping another run on banks.

In addition to his day job, Leland cleans and waxes the floors of the new Bayard Building. Edyth pulls in extra monies cooking in the St. Agnes Hospital kitchen. The previous week, she pawned her ruby earrings and gold necklace, but there's still no escaping foreclosure come April 30th. It is when Edyth thinks things can get no worse that Leland begins to hit her. She masks the bruises on her chin and wrists with make-up and powder. She throws the half-empty bottles of gin and wine in the trash—she knows his hiding places. He buys more, with money from where, she does not know. When he comes home plastered that Thursday night and demands intercourse, which she delicately refuses, he brandishes his belt and whips her, cornered between the curio cabinet and the dinette set, while she screams, huddled in a ball, her arms wrapped around her face, waking Benjamin in the upstairs nursery, who wails until he throws up.

Soon, Leland turns to his son Benjamin for pleasure, who has not yet turned one, fondling the boy's genitals, while he masturbates into Edyth's panties. When the boy grows, soon to turn two, he enters him from behind, leaving Benjamin raw, bloody and bruised. He forced himself down Benjamin's mouth, one time, until Benjamin turned faintly blue, while Leland, in a trance, had a flash memory of almost losing consciousness when sodomized by Dr. Fletcher.

When Benjamin turns fifteen, he flees, living on the streets, until he decides he'd rather live than die, and goes back to school, living in a safe house, applying for government handouts, planning and plotting his ultimate revenge: getting rich—making the kind of money that wields power.

Part Nine

Chapter Twenty-Four

RED ROCK CANYON

SEDONA, ARIZONA, A TWO-AND-A-HALF hour drive north from Celia's home, is known as a New Age mecca. Celia pulls off at a lookout point as she approaches her destination. The landscape is otherworldly—towering mountain spires and canyons of red rock against a crystal blue sky. Four million visitors each year descend upon this strange desert land—some of the most breathtaking scenery in the world, her guidebook touted. Legend has it, she read, that the ancient Indians honored Sedona as holy and that their ruins hold powerful spiritual energies.

She is traveling to attend a conference, called "Pilgrimage into Dreamtime," a two-day retreat as a journey to "meet your animal totem"— of special interest to Celia because of her affinity for animals. She saw a flyer at her yoga studio for this spiritual conference over Memorial Day weekend, and as it turned out, the Petersons and their daughter Lauren (in Cosette's seventh grade class), invited Cosette to join them for the long weekend at their summer house in La Jolla. Clay would be traveling through Saturday afternoon for business.

Celia's impromptu trip is a celebration of further success with her paintings. Ed Orinston, who takes pride in helping guide the careers of the artists whose work he collects, encouraged her to seek gallery representation beyond Arizona. Celia was aware that getting a gallery to show her paintings in California or New Mexico would be the right next step and, if she could pull it off, a coup. After many months of no responses and curt, confidence-draining notes of rejection to the images of her paintings sent to many galleries, she landed a deal with a relatively new art space in Santa Fe. This recognition prompted Celia to think that apart from being Clay's wife and Cosette's mother, she was someone all her own. The gallery almost doubled her prices and over the month of her show, sold many of her paintings. She had decided to celebrate by taking a weekend trip.

...

There are twenty attendees, who meet in a yoga studio nestled in Boynton Canyon, one of the most picturesque spots in all of Sedona. The teacher, Adelair Post, with kinky red hair swept up in a silver barrette, wearing a saffron dress with a crimson sash, instructs everyone to take a blanket from a pile in the back of the room.

"Your animal totem will reveal distinct qualities to you," she announces, as Celia spreads her blanket and gets comfortable in a prone position, at her teacher's instruction. Beige linen curtains are drawn against the noon sun and candles are lit around the perimeter of the room. Adelair beats a small drum, at first slowly, then faster, in a rhythm that reminds Celia of a heartbeat. On her back, her eyes closed, Celia's eyes begin pulsing, a kind of vibrating, which Adelair describes to the group as waking REM (rapid eye movement). Slipping into waking dreamtime, Celia is transported to a lake. Kneeling at the water's edge, she gazes at willow trees swaying overhead, the swooping branches skimming the top of the blue-green water. "Just let your imagination take you—follow your own path," encourages Adelair, as Celia senses the approach of what seems like a large fish. Then, out of the water, emerges a crocodile. *A crocodile! This is my totem?* She's horrified. *Why can't I have a swan or a dolphin or something furry and cuddly like a rabbit or a cat,* she frets.

The rhythmic drumming gets louder and faster—deep, resonating beats that fill her head. As Celia's thoughts and judgments clear, she sees her crocodile fully emerge and slither onto land, its broad, clawed feet and short, scaly legs moving along the shore. She thinks she'll be scared, but is in awe of its power, its versatility—swimming beneath water, walking on land. Even the mud along the shoreline takes on meaning, allowing life to grow in moist, dark places. The crocodile seems a master of its surroundings for the paramount goal—survival.

As the drumbeat slows and Adelair rings high-pitched bells, Celia is pulled out of her dream and back into the room. When she opens her eyes, Adelair is smiling at the students, encouraging them to share their experiences. Several people raise their hands and Adelair calls on each one. A pretty brunette seated behind Celia says, "I was an eagle flying over mountains."

"Ah, the eagle," Adelair enthusiastically exclaims. "To certain Native American tribes, the eagle controls thunder and rain, retribution and reward. The eagle has great spiritual powers. To accept an eagle totem, you must learn to spread healing and bring new creative forces into the world." Celia feels deflated, thinking, I am the spiritual equivalent of a ferocious reptile.

A bearded man across the room wearing all white shares, "I was a tiger roaming the jungle."

"If a tiger is your totem," advises Adelair, "expect new adventures and new passions in your life."

Next, a tall young woman with close-cropped blond hair and dangling silver earrings says, "This is kind of embarrassing, but, I was, well, an ass." She laughs and the group joins her in laughter. Admiring her honesty, Celia considers sharing her animal totem.

"Most people associate your animal totem with negative qualities," explains Adelair, "but the ass appears in Medieval Art as a symbol of patience and humility. With this totem, you might ask yourself if you're displaying appropriate humility."

Celia feels sorry for the ass girl and wonders whether she should keep silent or share her totem. Raising her hand and with a blush rising to her face, she finds herself speaking to the group.

"Ah, our friend the crocodile," responds Adelair. Celia feels a rush of relief by her teacher's reply. "On land, the crocodile is low to the ground—grounded in existence. In water, the crocodile's eyes—high on its head—secretly emerging above the surface, scouts for danger and food. The crocodile is deft in both domains. To accept this totem, you take responsibility for your own life. Women who tend to relinquish their power to men can use this lesson from the crocodile." Celia feels exposed.

Cringing, she listens to Adelair continue, dropping her head so no one can see her face. "You may recognize another teaching of your totem…when the crocodile's eggs develop enough to begin squeaking from the inside, the mother answers her young by gingerly carrying them in her mouth to the water. She is gentle and nurturing. Unlike most reptiles, the crocodile is an exceptional mother. You must be, too." Celia hesitantly lifts her chin and looks up at Adelair, who gives her a warm smile.

That evening, Celia orders Chinese take-out and eats her dinner propped against pillows in bed. She settles back and relaxes, thinking about what Adelair said. *Have I relinquished my power to men, to Clay? Did Adelair's interpretation of my animal totem make sense?* She concludes that she often feels unsafe in the world, needing Clay to make her feel secure. She feels that being married, having a man, grants certification that she's with the program, part of the norm; it's a stamp of approval, a statement that she has a protector, is worthy of one. She even felt nervous about taking the trip to Sedona, all on her own, having lost the adventuress Celia, who navigated four years in Manhattan. But even then, she envisioned marriage, pairing herself with a man who would hold a lamp and brandish a sword, ushering her along in a man's world. She thought about the popular women's lib books she'd read that came out in the seventies and eighties—about the strides women made, and she did see the progress. Women headed corporations, filled increasingly higher percentages of spots in medical and law schools, rose to leadership in politics, but it sure seemed as if many of the more subtle discriminations remained, just more artfully veiled. Good jobs are accessible, but the positions are governed by the rules at hand, a man's rules, which fuel the greed, the corruption, she felt. To get ahead, women must quell their nurturing instincts, deny the heart, lead with the head. And who in this construct is raising the children? Who's at home?

she wonders. She recalls having lunch earlier that day with a group at the conference. The bearded man wearing all white introduced himself to her—Brett was his name—asking, "So, what do you do?" Celia replied, "I'm an artist, a painter," feeling for the first time a sense of victory and legitimacy, because raising a daughter, no matter how noble, doesn't provide means to make your way in the world. She pulls up the covers; turns out the light. She doesn't know what to make of it all.

The following day entails guest lecturers and group meditations and Brett sits next to her, dressed in all white—again. She can't decide if this is an affectation or if she kind of likes it. He wears white painter's pants and a white linen, hippie-style shirt. On his wrist dangle silver and leather bracelets and on his hand—no wedding ring. He smiles at her as they chat before class begins, and she wonders if he's actually coming on to her. Could this be? Yes, it could. She's forgotten what it feels like. It feels good. There's an appeal to him, although he might not be described as handsome. He's certainly younger than she is, she calculates, and recalls that he said he's a magazine journalist.

They take a short walk into town at day's end to grab a bite for dinner and along the way, he recounts his immersion in all things New Age. He's been to India on a six-month pilgrimage to meet various gurus and taken a class in San Francisco about the healing properties of crystals—showing Celia an oblong crystal on a long, black cord around his neck, which he fishes out from under his shirt and has Celia hold to "feel the vibration." He's been a vegetarian for almost ten years and does 30-day juice fasts each spring and his yoga practice is quite advanced. Suddenly, Celia feels like a failure. He's the New Age quarterback and she hasn't made the team.

He wants to stop into a little shop next to the restaurant before it closes, called Metaphysical Manifestations, where he buys a sage stick and incense, which he'll burn "to clear out the energies in my hotel room," he says. Celia looks around the store, while he sorts out his purchase. There are crystals and tarot cards and little tables set up in the back, so customers can have psychic readings. Books about angels and astrology line the back wall. Feathered dream catchers and other beaded Native American souvenirs are displayed on tables. The silver and turquoise jewelry looks cheap and tacky. The tired woman behind the counter has on some kind of feathered headdress and smeared red lipstick that makes her look like a cockatoo. Celia feels a little lightheaded and then, an enormous wave of anxiety floats in…this whole New Age thing is a hoax. She's been had. Her meditations are complete fantasy. She's made everything up. Adelair has hoodwinked her and given a bogus class for cash. She has to get out of the store. She says she'll meet him next door at the café.

Her meal goes untouched, as she listens to Brett make himself out to be a highly evolved soul, who scores more points for heaven than the average Joe. He's a talker and when she realizes she can simply tune out, for even her polite nods and little phrases of recognition to his stories go unnoticed, she takes deep breaths and comes to her senses, realizing that even though some folks market God like items in an airport gift shop and there is a lot of arrogance around the pursuit of the Divine, it doesn't deny the validity of her spiritual practice; it doesn't negate her own strides.

When they get back to their cars and Brett asks if she wants to watch the stars from the terrace off his room, she does something terribly rude. She laughs—it just comes up and out, and then profusely apologizes which doesn't make it any better.

. . .

The following day seems like a present to Celia: not one thing on her schedule and the beauty of Sedona beckoning at her doorstep. She decides to avoid town altogether—too commercial—and hike Boynton Canyon, which she read in her guide book is a site of spiritual significance, a vortex, a swirling center of energy emanating from Earth's surface, similar to those found at Stonehenge in England, the Great Pyramids in Egypt, and other sacred spots around the globe. Sacred sites, she read, have transformational powers that can promote spiritual growth and awaken compassion, wisdom and reverence for the planet.

Boynton Canyon is among the most popular vortex sites in Sedona—including Cathedral Rock, Bell Rock, and Chapel Rock. She chooses it because the guidebook says each site has a specific energy—feminine, masculine, or both—and Boynton Canyon is touted as infusing the masculine. Considering the message of her animal totem, she concludes it's an optimum excursion for the day, which is sunny and windy, the sky stretching wide, offering the heavens. Along the trail, she sees hibiscus, red fairy dusters, and aloe—pale green spikes tipped with blossoms of orange. The bright pink bougainvillea and the vivid purple lantana beeline to her brain, like opiates. When she tires, she sits cross-legged in the shadow of a tall tree, atop a warm rock, pulling up the energies of Mother Earth, spinning them upward toward her heart, then her head, then taking the potent light from above and integrating it into her energy field. These are skills she practiced with her tapes, which she can now employ on her own.

As Celia becomes more sensitive to the energies surrounding her, she is challenged keeping the darker resonances out of her field. It's as if her skin is overly porous, so while she can sense and pull in beauty and light, it also leaves her more sensitive to negativity. When she returns home in the late afternoon, Clay is curt with her, angry she's been away. Yet, Celia reacts not in her usual way—trying to win him back by serving his needs ever more diligently, but by disengaging from the scene—taking a hot bath until Cosette returns. This small act of self-care is emancipating. During her three-day absence, dishes have piled up in the sink and on the counters, damp towels litter the bathroom floor, the weekend's mail (bills, letters and catalogs), and crusty dishes and beer bottles, are strewn across the den. She amusingly recalls The Wolf's cat, Frida, who used to pee in his bed when he went away for a couple of days to show The Wolf who's boss.

...

The following week, Ed Orinston commissions Celia to do a painting for his New York apartment—to replace a painting by another artist that he's sold. Celia embraces the project with enthusiasm. Thoroughly engrossed in her work one afternoon, she forgets to pick up Cosette from her SAT study group at 5:30. Cosette calls and says, "Mom—you OK? You're always early." Celia apologizes and hops in the car. But, Clay is angry at the dinner table that night yelling, "first things first" and "responsibility of a parent," as both Celia and Cosette lower their gazes, enduring his rant. This kind of thing happens more frequently now and they've learned the best tactic—let it pass over.

The painting is ready in a couple of months and Ed is effusive—he loves it. Before he hangs the canvas in the living room of his Upper East Side apartment, he takes it over to Paul Booth's gallery, without Celia's knowledge, to give the dealer a look—thinking Booth just might take her on, represent her work. Turning 68 that year, Booth is still New York's consummate art dealer and he looks the part—elegant European suit, signature polka dot tie, small round tortoise shell glasses, straight hair parted on the side, slicked back, dyed black. He seems younger than his years, due to two face lifts. He's on his fourth wife; they got younger as he gets older. Penelope, his latest, a stunning French model, who touts herself as a former actress because she did a television commercial a few years back, runs the gallery now, a full-time nanny at home with their twin boys. Few people like Booth—he is immensely arrogant, but nobody would dare refute his eye.

Booth studies Celia Barrens' painting propped on a display easel, while seated on a black leather couch, sipping Perrier with lime in "the back room," where all deals—both buying and selling—take place. He is silent for a long time. Ed construes he wants some space, so he wanders the gallery, watching Harlan Lee Wolfe and a small crew cart The Wolf's paintings through, in preparation for his upcoming show. Ed has been one of The Wolf's few champions over the years. Remaining in town for a few days on business, Ed tells The Wolf he'll be there for the opening. "Terrific," he says, distracted by managing his crew, but wanting to schmooze Ed, who he hopes might buy some of his new work.

"Seems I know a former student of yours," says Ed.

"Yeah, who's that?" replies The Wolf, carrying a large wrapped canvas through the gallery.

"Celia Barrens. Turns out, I bought some of her work."

The Wolf stops in his tracks, sets the painting against the wall, wipes his brow with his sleeve and cautiously looks up at Ed. "No kidding," he says, buying time, not knowing how to respond, wondering if Ed knows she's the kid in the portrait he sold him, wondering where the fuck this conversation is going.

"Saw her work in a second-rate Scottsdale gallery, but it's good, damn good. Now she's showing in Santa Fe and I've brought a piece in to show Booth. I think she might have something, but Booth's been in there with it a long time, probably too long."

A burly guy from The Wolf's crew, carrying a large canvas off the truck, yells out, "Where's this one go?"

"Bring it through here," says The Wolf.

"Don't want to distract you—see you at the opening," says Ed.

When The Wolf hears Penelope summon Booth to the front desk to say hello to a client, The Wolf ducks into the back room to sneak a peek at Celia's painting. It hits him like a brick. The power is undeniable. It's good. Too good.

He quickly cuts out, directing the crew to move the truck out of the loading dock and finishes stacking his paintings in the storage room, ready to hang on Wednesday for the Thursday night opening. The show will run the month of April, the height of New York's spring season and The Wolf isn't going to let anything or anyone stop him from his long overdue bask in the limelight. He's waited half his career for the return of realism. His painting style, after two decades' of neglect, is finally inching back into vogue and the resentment he harbors for all the years he's missed recognition and success, due to the whims of the fickle art market, has brewed to a boil. He's getting too old to teach and ever more impatient with the second-rate students who pass through his classes, year after year, their parents footing the outrageous tuition. His muses no longer interest him the way they used to. He chews them up and spits them out faster and faster, bedding them once their portraits are barely complete, sending them hastily on their way to make way for a new conquest, frantically reviving his lust to fuel his faltering artistic inspiration. Certainly, no former conquest of his, just another privileged pussy whose parents paved her path with gold, should build a fast career, should be spared the suffering he's endured.

The Wolf overhears Booth talking to Ed in the front room. "You might have found a hot wire here, Ed, with this girl. I want to see more. Get me three or four paintings. Have her send them overnight—I'll foot the cost."

When Ed calls Celia with the news, Celia is stunned. "Paul Booth?" she mumbles. "Really? Paul Booth is interested in my work?" She has three paintings to send—one is a personal favorite, which hangs in her living room, two are recently finished and still in her studio.

Just as he calculated, The Wolf is hanging his show when Celia's shipment arrives two days later, figuring one day for packing, one day for transit. His scheme, if he can put it swiftly into place, is already under way. He has asked Priscilla Meade, his senior student, to leave a few "choice" paintings of hers at school—under the guise of showing them to a dealer, who might be interested in her work. Oh, how The Wolf hates Prissy's contrived use of color, the void of anything authentic in her work, but her abstract style and painterly application is ideal…close enough to Celia's canvases, but missing anything resembling the passion that inspires a true artist's work. But can he switch them—replace Celia's paintings with Prissy's—under Penelope's keen nose? As long as she's distracted up front, he doesn't see why not. Booth is almost always entertaining a client over lunch at New York's latest hot spot—early afternoon just might work.

As The Wolf suspected, Booth is out mid-day and Penelope is busy with a customer—a Japanese man on business in New York. The Japanese are buying up big-ticket contemporary canvases like crazy and Penelope is doing her best dog and pony show, completely distracted, as The Wolf, with a confident and quick step, carries Prissy's work concealed in wrap, straight through the gallery's front door, Penelope assuming the paintings are part of his show. In the silent storage room, he quickly exchanges the paintings in the shipping boxes and slides Celia's work behind a crate. Could it be this simple? He laughs out loud, driving back to his apartment. All that's required now is another switch after Booth has a look, no doubt Prissy's paintings will never make the cut.

After Ian, the gallery intern, unloads the boxes and places what are supposedly Celia's paintings on display easels in the back room, at Booth's direction, Booth positions himself with high anticipation on the smooth leather couch to have a look. His thin lips curl under, his nostrils flare, his hand reaches to his mouth as if he's eaten spoiled fish. "Ian, get this *trash* out of my sight," he yells out. Booth is quite sensitive to what's placed within his vision. Bad art actually turns his stomach. "Ian, tout suite," he shouts, "before I barf."

. . .

That evening, at the opening party for The Wolf's exhibition, amid the bustle of New York's chicest crowd, The Wolf casually asks Booth what he thought of his former student's work, gauging if Booth already viewed the paintings. Lifting his hand in a flamboyant gesture and pinching the end of his nose, as if avoiding a putrid stench, Booth hisses, "Spare me the *dregs* of the earth."

Exiting the gallery's main exhibition space, chuckling to himself, The Wolf discreetly enters the storage facility and deftly maneuvers the second and final switch—putting Celia's paintings back in their boxes. The following day, with just a little finesse—saying he's left several of his canvases in the storage room—he loads Prissy's paintings into his van on the loading dock, as a letter is printed and signed on the heavy-stock, pale purple stationary of the Paul Booth Gallery that Celia's work is "unsuitable for representation." As it happens, on that same morning that Celia receives the dreadful letter, The Wolf informs Priscilla Meade that he hasn't shown her paintings after all, saying that the dealer changed his mind about viewing students' work. Priscilla, who already holds a certain disdain for her teacher, thinks, *you worm.*

Celia does not suspect that this rejection will send her into a fast-descending spiral. Soliciting Booth, after all, is just reaching too high, she tells herself, Ed simply too enthusiastic, she concludes, or maybe also self-serving, since moving forward the careers of the artists he collects increases the prestige and value of their work. But, her creative output comes to a grinding halt. She tries hiding her change in mood from Clay, for her vulnerability, she has learned, fuels his increasingly frequent recriminations. During the past year, he's vacillated between icily remote and argumentative, finding fault in her every move. Nothing she does pleases him, so she distances herself, in the aim of self-protection. Her slump lasts almost a month. When she's had enough self-punishment, she turns to her meditation practice to assuage her grief.

She realizes that the spiritual progress she makes is always prompted by nothing other than desperation. Suffering really is the catalyst for change, she thinks, dejectedly. *Stubborn—that's what I am.* Only when cornered does she turn to the spiritual realm. Increasing the frequency with which she plays her tapes, she begins shifting her mood. Day by day, things get brighter, until she perceives the rebuff of her paintings in a broader perspective. Her worth, she concludes, must come from her own assessment of herself, of her creative output. This realization spills over, revealing insights into her relationship with Clay. She'll never pull herself up if she lets him determine her value, she decides. Sadly, he seems intent on bringing her down. It becomes increasingly clear that he's threatened by her making her way in the world, by the woman she's growing into, instead of the frightened girl she's been.

. . .

The following morning, when Clay leaves for a two-day trip to Dallas to evaluate a land purchase and it coincides with Cosette's school trip to Washington, DC, Celia impulsively plans a visit back to Sedona. A short sojourn seems an ideal way to fuel her stirring creative spirit. She envisions hiking and sketching the red rock mountains, then meditating under a moonlit sky.

Pulling over to stop at a lookout point, Celia unwraps her avocado, sprout and provolone sandwich and takes in the view of saguaros spotting the desert valley below and the red rock mountains of Sedona, in the distance, calling her forward on her journey north. There are only two picnic tables and she's reluctant to take a seat, for one is occupied by a large, boisterous family with a fussy toddler. At the only other table, a lone man wears a ski hat and down vest, even though the temperature is over ninety. So, she remains in her car, the engine cut, the radio on low, tuned to National Public Radio. A playwright is being interviewed, who wrote a play called *Sins of the Father*. "One in four girls will be sexually abused before they turn 18," she's saying, "35% by a family member." Celia thinks she must have misunderstood. This seems impossible. "And in families you'd least expect," the playwright continues. "This is not relegated to the fringes. I grew up in a wealthy enclave of Long Island, in New York. My father—educated, successful, and a widower—sexually abused me, starting when I was four." Celia turns the dial to the classics rock station and listens to Crosby, Stills, Nash and Young, instead.

After spending the afternoon hiking to a Native American archeological site—the Palatki Ruins, a cliff dwelling built by Sinaqua Indians, Celia stops into a convenience store to buy more water, for she's had the last sip from her bottle. She lingers to overhear a conversation between two women in the next aisle, talking about a psychic that one had just seen. This intrigues Celia, who wonders if there's any validity to these professed sages, who claim to see the past, to read the future.

"No, I'm not joking. She even knew his name. How is that possible? I was totally freaked." Celia walks nearer to where the women stand, so she can hear better, but still hide in the adjacent aisle. "She knew he died—and knew the month and year—April, 1971—and that it was a stroke. Really, I was shaking. It sort of gave me the creeps."

Celia hears the other woman ask, "What'd she say about Mitch?"

"Not so hot," she answers, dejectedly. "She called him a coyote, a trickster, said he's not trustworthy and that his music project, which you know is the record he's producing, isn't going to work out either. Basically, he's bad news. But, you know, I think, maybe, I kind of knew it, but didn't want to see it."

"Going in, I was like, jeez, this is probably a big waste of money," the woman continues, "but I was just floored. And, you know, her name—Joy Star—which she says is her real name, I thought, oh, come on."

After Celia purchases her water, she peruses the shop's bulletin board— and there it is—a small flyer tacked there: Psychic Joy Star. She puts the number in her cell phone, walks to the sidewalk, places a call and books an appointment for the following afternoon.

Take Lindsay Lane, Joy had said, until it curves left. Third house on your right: Number 12. Celia pulls up to a small white cottage with purple shutters in need of some serious repainting. An old Ford pickup, faded red and rusted out, and a motorcycle are parked in the narrow gravel driveway. Two large terracotta pots brimming with bright red geraniums flank the purple-painted door. As Celia is about to ring the bell, the door opens. Joy Star reminds Celia of Joni Mitchell in the sixties…tall, blonde hair to her waist with bangs, younger than she imagined—probably in her twenties— wearing a green silk dress with a V-neck and bell sleeves. "Come in, come in." Celia follows her inside, noting that she's barefoot. A gruff, good-looking guy with tattoos on his pronounced biceps seems to be leaving. Celia pairs him with the shiny Harley in the driveway. Joy ushers Celia into a small room, painted pale lavender, and offers her a seat on an antique settee. "Two minutes—be right with you," Joy smiles and rushes back into the foyer. Celia overhears Joy giggle, but can't discern their hushed conversation, and then, comes a silence that probably means kissing, before the front door shuts and Joy joins Celia.

Joy fans out her dress and takes a seat on a straight-backed wood chair, directly across from Celia, who sits on an overly ornate Victorian settee upholstered in a satiny purple fabric. Two dachshunds come trailing in, beautiful dogs with deep brown eyes and thick, lustrous coats. Joy giggles. "They have to be where the action is. If you like, I can…"

"Oh, no. It's fine." The dogs sniff Celia's shoes, then Celia helps them jump up to settle in next to her on her seat, reaching over to rub their foreheads and ears.

"Do you have something of yours I can hold?" asks Joy. Celia is confused. "Keys, sunglasses, a ring or any piece of jewelry. It tunes me into your energy—clues me into stuff I might not ordinarily get." Celia fishes for her sunglasses and retrieves them from her knapsack, feeling ashamed of her reluctance to hand over her wedding ring or watch, wondering if she'd get them back.

Joy places them in her lap and closes her eyes. Celia watches Joy's face for clues. At first, Joy is serene, but then her forehead wrinkles up in crooked lines and her mouth turns down. *Is this intense concentration or something terrible about to be told, an ominous fortune, a forewarning?* Joy sits like this for forever, it seems to Celia, although it's less than a minute. It occurs to Celia to leave. Whatever is about to be revealed, she doesn't want to know. When Joy opens her eyes, she gazes at Celia with enormous compassion. Celia sees tears well up in Joy's eyes.

In anticipation, Celia holds her breath. "I am about to undertake a kind of trance," says Joy, "after calling in guides that help me speak to you. Anything revealed today will be for your highest good, so have no fears. What I'm hearing, what I'm getting, is that much truth is about to come in. A truth you are finally ready to hear. This is your time, they are saying, to come into knowingness, for this knowledge will help you heal." Celia sits up straight and clasps her hands in her lap. Her palms are sweating.

Joy's glossy eyes light up in excitement. "Oh, we have quite the legion of angels here with us today," she says, looking around the room with a welcoming smile. Celia berates herself for wondering, *Am I sitting across from a certifiable lunatic?* "Your guide is here, too," Joy says, closing her eyes again, making a contented humming sound, as if she's just tasted a delicious dessert. "I am receiving greetings from Paramahansa Yogananda." Astonished, Celia's stares at Joy, who sits with her back straight, her eyes closed, a satisfied smile across her face. "OK, then," Joy continues, reciting what seems like a rehearsed speech, the words trailing fast: "Today, we host ascended masters and saints in the highest good of Celia Barrens, all sentient beings on the planet Earth and the universe. On this auspicious day, she will receive information of the highest order to assist her soul in its inevitable journey home. Let it be so." Joy pauses here. Then, as if receiving a fax from God, she nods and reports, "So it is."

After a minute or two of unbearable silence, Joy begins speaking in a soft monotone: "I see your father. A soul in pain. A soul who returned to source through an act of violence." Celia feels a sickening stirring in her stomach. "Did you father take his life?" asks Joy.

"Yes," says Celia, tears welling up in her eyes.

Joy says, "I see a gun…is that…was it…?"

Celia swallows hard and says, "Yes."

"It was an act of grace," Joy continues, her chin now lifted high, her forehead tilted up toward the ceiling, her back arched. "He is not in a bad place. He spared your life for his. Yet, he has caused you great pain through heinous acts. Your forgiveness of his crimes against you will come when the time is ripe, unfolding like the blossoming of a flower. I see a rose, a pink rose, a closed bud. It will bloom. The fragrance is sharp, but sweet." Celia is crying now. She fishes for a tissue in her knapsack and finds a paper napkin, which she uses to blot her nose and cheeks. The dogs jump down and scurry off.

"He carried a dark, destructive energy." Tears slowly slip from Joy's closed lids and slide down her face, as she says, "You are small, an infant. It is hard for you to breathe, to get air. He is forceful, out of himself, out of control. He enters you. This is abuse of a sexual nature. It is violence. It is the color black, a blue-black and also dark green, a murky green. Here, here…we have Yogananda saying, 'Be strong, dear one, this dawning of light upon a dark time is part of a greater plan. Let it be. We value your courage and strength, more than you know. You are not abandoned. You

155

are not forsaken, as you fear. You are not punished for sins, as you have imagined. You are love, a love as bright as the sun, capable of helping transmute dark forces."

Convulsing in deep sobs, Celia's thoughts spiral: *How could this be? How could he? Should I believe this?* Words swirl in her head like swarming bees: *Dirty, bad girl, father, shame, sin, sullied.*

Joy is quiet for a few moments; she bows her head, then lifts it skyward again, continuing: "Your soul reaches for creative release. It is your blueprint to create, to create with pencils and paper and paint. Your surrender to this desire gives you peace, great peace and solace. Activities of this kind should be honored now; time relegated to these pursuits." Joy slowly raises both her hands, palms facing out, then gently places them back in her lap. "I see a child, yes? Your child? A girl. She is almost grown. You have kept her from harm, stopped short, so to speak, in its tracks, the forces of destruction. Yet, you carry fear for her safety and we want to assure you, she is safe. You have bestowed upon her the greatest gift, unconditional love, which she will carry into the world. She is among many children who will help heal Earth, in dire need of resurrection. I also see a tall, handsome man. He is, how do you say, candy to the eye? Yes? But, not sweet to the taste. He is double-dealing, slippery like a shark. I see the letter 'C.' Is it Carl? Or, no…is it the letter 'K?' I cannot see or hear his name, which is one syllable. Does this…is this?"

"This is my hus…husband…Clay," Celia sobs.

"His spark of light is deeply hidden," says Joy. "You knowingly live under his shadow, an oppression which diminishes your light, your essence. You will come to embrace this slowly, within the right time. Your power will ultimately not be denied. You will remember who you are. Amen."

Joy takes a deep breath and opens her eyes, finding Celia curled in a fetal position, her sweatshirt balled under her head, rocking back and forth, trying to contain her tears. Joy kneels at the couch and strokes Celia's hair, like a mother attending her sick child, repeating her name, softly, compassionately, "Celia, Celia," and then, saying again, to assuage her pain and fear, "You will remember who you are."

In perfect harmony, their voices chiming like synchronized bells, Lady Kamara exclaims, "You will remember who you are."

Celia drives straight to Boynton Canyon to be alone, to meditate, to somehow stop this feeling that she is tumbling down, falling into a hole. A horn blares behind her; she realizes she's stopped at a light, now green. She pulls over, mops her face with her sweatshirt, wet from tears, and composes herself to drive. At the canyon, she pulls on her hiking boots, which she's left in the car. Slumped over and shuffling, she walks and walks. *Just think... just get your thoughts straight. Can I get my thoughts straight ever again?*

At first, she seeks denial. *It simply isn't true.* Her father could not have, would not have...but this rationale doesn't stand up against the uncanny accuracy of the reading, she concludes, recalling Joy intuiting the presence of her guide, Paramahansa Yogananda, her father's suicide—even the gun. *What else? What else?* Her mind races...her drawings and paintings, that she has a child, a girl, almost grown, that she worries too much about her, that her husband is handsome—*and what was that last part? What was that about? What is he up to that I don't know about? Is he as dark as Joy said?* This scares her, but not as much as the idea that she's been molested by her own father. It's all too much, too much to absorb, too much to bear. *And what was that all about on the radio on the way up? That snippet I heard on the talk show about sexual abuse.* The synchronicity is eerie, makes her knees go weak, her legs shake.

What is the truth? How can I be sure? She thinks to ask her mother, but Celia fears her mother will quickly dismiss her—the information gathered from a psychic in Sedona, or more likely, be outraged, interpreting the inquiry as an accusation.

If only Maggie was alive. During the years following her departure (when Celia turned ten), leaving to care for a newborn in an Annapolis family, Celia had kept in touch by making and mailing Christmas cards and calling each year on Easter and her birthday. It was during her first year at college that Celia received the letter (along with the returned Christmas card), from Maggie's employer saying that Maggie died of pancreatic cancer. Celia was devastated at the loss, regretful that she'd never visited, wishing, at the very least, that she'd had a chance to say goodbye.

Without any other recourse, Celia asks for a sign. She asks to see her favorite bird—a hummingbird. If she sees one, her psychic reading will be true. She reclines on the warm rocks and looks into the vast stretch of blue sky for her little, fast, fluttering bird and tries to focus on her breath. *Just breathe. Try to relax.* She does—she's calmer. She hikes back to the car and heads to the hotel, all the while looking for her sign. Less agitated, she's suddenly hungry. She hasn't eaten all day. Stopping at a café, she orders a bowl of fresh fruit, a blueberry muffin and lemonade. She'll eat, head back to her room, take a long, hot shower—wash away this dreadful day—get into her nightgown, get into bed and sleep. She needs sleep. She sits by the window, her face a bruised peach, eyes swollen from tears, focusing her gaze outside. And then, a small miracle....there it is, a hummingbird hovering right outside the window, just as the waitress places her meal on the table. "Oh, look, look!" the waitress says, pointing. "A hummingbird. Been working this place a year—first time I've seen one." Celia starts to cry. A very odd response, thinks the waitress, who takes a step back and tries not to stare. Bowing her head, Celia asks her to pack up the meal and drives back to the hotel, where she falls onto the bed and drifts straight away into sleep. In the early morning, half-awake, she recalls only fleeting images of her dreams: She stands before the mirror in the girl's bathroom at her high school, reaching under her hair to unlatch a necklace, but terrifyingly finds a snake coiled around her neck. Then, she's swimming to a boat in a murky lake. As she approaches, exhausted, she sees it's an open coffin. Panting, she pulls herself up to look inside expecting to see her father, but the corpse is her. She reaches inside and surprisingly, rouses the dead body.

...

A door left locked for 39 years is ajar. It is a room of the darkest secrets, of unspeakable sins, of a betrayal of the most treacherous sort. Celia peers inside. It is a furtive glance, but it takes all that she is to face this fear, to look beyond the door, to see the past as it is, not as she wishes. Her feelings ride a wave. Some days she manages floating, other days she capsizes, not knowing if or when she'll come up for air. Her despair, hard as she tries, cannot be concealed. Clay recognizes, even relishes this sinking of her ship, but offers no inquiries about her state. *How can a father hurt his child?* She wonders. *Why would a husband hurt his wife—the mother of his child?* She can't fathom it.

Concerned, Cosette asks what's wrong. Celia only shares that she's going through a hard time, a transition of sorts that will take some time to turn around. One day, she tells Cosette, she will share more. Celia takes long walks. She takes long baths. Sometimes, she excuses herself early from dinner before dessert with tales of headaches or fatigue. She devotes herself to one thing: reading. She reads furtively—from books carefully tucked beneath sweaters and quilts—books about physical and sexual abuse, incest and betrayal.

For Cosette, her mother's process holds relatively little consequence, for she is poised for autonomy, almost out the door, like most seniors in high school. She has her boyfriend, her Toyota, her own busy schedule of school and clubs, and a part-time job. College is around the corner. She hardly feels the wind swirling, only faintly hears the rustling of the leaves in the trees from the escalating force of Celia's wrath, the inevitable rise of her anger. And the storm is not headed for her. It's beelining for Clay. But, he's a tough match and he isn't going to lose one inch of footing in the game he's perfected, the power game, even up against evidence of his infidelity, as clear as a sun-drenched day.

Chapter Twenty-Five

VERONICA

CLAY IS IN THE SHOWER WHEN his cell phone rings. Celia walks over and watches the light flash: Veronica Halsey 480-744-2290. *Why is some woman calling him on his cell Saturday morning at eight?* She picks up the phone. She hesitates. She listens to the message.

"Shit. I can't make it," the voice says. "Scott's back early and planned this birthday thing. I just can't get out of. I'll fly out tomorrow—first thing. There's a flight at six. I can stay 'til Monday—it's still two days. I'm like a cat in heat, here. Rrrrr. See you tomorrow, naughty boy. Call me ASAP."

A moment after Celia replaces the phone, sick to her stomach and trembling, Clay exits the bathroom, running late, dressing in a hurry, pulling on a navy Ralph Lauren polo and khaki pants, slipping into his Ferragamo loafers, while closing the clasp on his Rolex. He tosses a few last minute items into his leather duffle, zips it and places it by the bedroom door. He slips his matching wallet into his back pocket, his keys in his front pocket— and then, a long pause, stopping in his tracks. He looks at Celia, who sits in bed propped against pillows pretending to read, but scrutinizing his every move. He looks panicked, pale. He's a keen player, who doesn't miss a move. He knows. Something is up. Way up. He turns to her, "Have you seen my cell?"

Celia has not yet determined what she'll do, but she knows one thing for sure—he is not walking out of that room. And not with his cell phone. And she knows one more thing—she is terrified, but also furious. This betrayal by her husband of 18 years brings with it the betrayal of her father. It has a force that surprises her, that usurps her fear.

"Let's talk about Veronica Halsey," she blurts out, her accusatory eyes burning into Clay's, who averts her gaze.

"Celia, I'm running late—I'll miss my plane. Tell me what you did with my cell? Where is it? I've gotta go."

"No."

"Stop playing games."

He walks toward her, pulls the covers back, scans the bed. "Where is it? Cut it out."

"Tell me who she is. I have a right to know."

"What the hell? Fuckin' Christ—you're crazy. Sick in the head. Hysterical. She's a real estate agent. Whatever. She's nobody. I've got to run." Celia sits silently. "OK. Fine. I'm outta here. Back Monday." He turns and walks to the door, picks up his bag.

"Goodbye naughty boy," says Celia.

Clay turns, stunned. Then, his expression becomes vicious, angry. He looks like a bull dog.

"You are so busted, Clay Cutter." Celia is surprised at her own voice. Is it coming from her? She seems on autopilot, out of control. "Your *friend* left you a message, which I heard. I can't *believe* this. How long has this been going on?" She grabs the cell phone, which she tucked behind her, behind the pillow, and throws it, hard. It hits his knee. She's fuming, enraged. He scoops it up from the floor and brings it to his ear, his face red. Staring straight at Celia, he listens, expressionless.

"You drove me to this," he screams at her. "Who could live with you? Always in your studio."

"Don't turn this on me. That's so unfair. You're sleeping with another woman. Who is she? Do you love her? What the hell is going on?" Celia feels the room spinning. She doesn't want to hear his answers.

Clay tries composing himself. He stuffs his hands deep in his pants pocket, circles the room, assessing the situation, calculating his next move.

"Jesus fucking Christ," he mutters. His rage turns to Veronica for calling, to his own lax standards for stupidly leaving his cell by the bed. *So fucking stupid.*

He needs time to build a story, to get his facts straight, to manage damage control. He winces before turning to her. Can he say this convincingly? "Look, no, of course I don't love her. It means nothing to me. It's new—just few weeks. It's nothing. I love you. It's you I love."

Celia stops crying and looks up at him. He hasn't said he loved her in over a year. She wants to believe it. She wants things back the way they were—so many years ago. What happened to that Clay? Is he still in there?

"Really?"

He walks toward the bed, sits on the edge, puts his hand on her ankle. She can't help it, she pulls away. "Just thinking of you…of you with…"

"It's OK." They sit in silence looking at the floor. Clay's thoughts turn to his collapsed weekend plans. He wonders how he'll keep the affair going now. Celia suggests marriage counseling. Clay won't hear of it.

Late that evening, he calls Veronica, tells her what went down, says he needs a couple of days to "straighten things out," but he knows one thing for sure—there's no way he's stopping his afternoon trysts just to appease his nagging wife.

For the first time, Celia seriously questions whether or not she wants to stay with him, stay in the marriage. *What's left? Can I trust him? Do I love him?* Soon, the excuse "stay together for the sake of the child," will no longer apply. With Cosette's fellowship in California slated for June—volunteering at a kids' crisis center, and then off to college in late August, Celia knows it's best, for Cosette's sake, to keep things as pleasant as possible for the next six months and then, see where things go. Of late, she's seen so many marriages fall apart, empty nesters finding that the void filled by kids—once off to college—leaves a black hole. Is she inching toward that abyss?

Meditating about the fate of the relationship late into the evening, she knows she stays with Clay for one compelling reason: fear. The real "f" word…fear of being alone, fear of change, fear of getting back out there to find someone new to fill the emptiness, to ease the loneliness. She's ashamed of her revelation. She condemns herself for her lack of courage. She's also sorted out so much more about her past and how it's affected her present. The books she's recently devoured showed her that while her father's assaults marked her life almost 40 years ago, she's still a prisoner of her childhood. To escape this pain, she employed a dissociate defense that makes it impossible for her to accurately assess threats. If she cannot see the truth in herself; she cannot see the truth in others. She's also learned that until she comes face to face with the real events of her past, she'll reenact her victimhood. Childhood trauma, one of the books said, amplifies gender typecasts: Men with a history of childhood abuse tend to take out their aggression on others, while women with a history of childhood abuse are more likely to injure themselves or position themselves for victimization. Chapter after chapter told her story, as if her own life was on the page…women who've been sexually abused—especially in early childhood by a trusted figure, such as a father, exhibit promiscuity in adolescence, suffer from depression, think of suicide. Some try to kill themselves; others "succeed," the book said. A heartbreaking word choice, she remembered thinking.

Yet, in all this, she also found a glimmer of hope and forgiveness for herself, at last, an explanation for much of the pain she's carried, the ways she's acted out. What also becomes clearer is her understanding of a phrase she's read over and over again in just about every self-help or spiritual book promising happiness. A directive that seemed preposterous to her: Love yourself. *How does one go about this lofty goal? Where does one begin when the evidence of one's deeds and thoughts goes against this esoteric decree?* But, here, finally, she's come upon a clue: You don't have to be perfect, or anywhere near perfect, to feel self-love. You simply have to do your best, see yourself for who you are, love yourself for where you are on the path to whatever healing is required to become whole. Loving oneself means accepting oneself with all one's inevitable flaws. And, in doing so, that love, a genuine feeling of unconditional acceptance, is extended to others.

. . .

"Flowers, just for being you," says Clay, as Celia lifts the cardboard top off the long box, revealing two dozen long-stemmed yellow roses tied tight with a stiff yellow ribbon. She wants to be happy about this. He's trying. This is lovely, really, she tells herself, fake smiling at him behind cautious eyes, as she fills a large vase with water and pushes the thorned stems, one by one, inside. He's home more, too. He asks her about her day, about her paintings, about Cosette. He says he "wants to make things right." Little by little, he eases her fears, she lets down her guard, she thinks, maybe, I can trust him.

He assures her that he's broken off the affair. Yet, Clay is plotting his course, securing his options, and one thing is royally pissing him off—this monitoring of his comings and goings. As the weeks progress, Clay feels increasingly trapped, a tiger in a cage. He won't live like this—under her suspicious little thumb. Judgments and condemnations are intolerable; admiration is his lifeblood.

He does see less of Veronica, their meetings planned like bank heists— not the tiniest detail overlooked to ensure his secrets. Veronica feels slighted and tension develops there, too, prompting Clay's sights to stray to a newer, nicer, younger someone, who'll look up at him adoringly, who'll see him as he wants to see himself: the charmer, the man in charge, the one who's been mistreated. A mortgage banker has caught his eye; this was already brewing. Heather Meeley is pretty hot, pretty hot indeed, mid-twenties, fresh material, fresh out of school. In Heather Meeley, he perceives that perfect mix of neediness and naiveté, a formula for servitude.

As he reels Celia back in over the next few months, professing his love, his regret, his willingness and eagerness to turn things around, he craftily funnels joint monies into his own accounts, hides assets in carefully constructed tax shelters, meets with tax and divorce attorneys, maneuvering his IRAs, stocks, bonds, and investment properties. He files for divorce in May, taking Heather for a week's stay in Palm Springs, while a courier service serves Celia the divorce papers. Stunned, Celia thinks there must be some mistake, then like a torrent it hits her—how cunningly she's been deceived.

After fury, regret and tears, she forces herself to take hold, demanding of herself: Be strong. This is for the best, she repeats, again and again, in her head. He's a brute, a liar, a cheat, a reenactment of my childhood, she furiously scribbles in her journal. And though she initially moves forward in a gray haze, a half-paralyzed robotic mode, she keeps her feet on the ground; her gaze on the road ahead. Some days, it works. Other days, she feels abandoned, rejected, and overwhelmed with trepidation.

...

Nancy Stutts, Celia's divorce attorney, removes her horn-rimmed glasses, pushes her chair back from her white wood desk and delivers the facts: "Half the house is yours," she says, "and there are *some* pension funds, but not much else. He's been, how shall I say, *astute*, in *shifting* things around." Nancy makes a sour face, here. "I'm afraid it's all legal though, and unless you take him to court—and I really can't give you much assurance of success—there's not a whole lot you can do." Celia slumps in her chair, takes a deep breath and waits for Nancy to continue. "Short term alimony is a given, but because you can work, I don't think we can expect much." Celia doesn't want to go to court. She calculates that with the cash from the house and the trickle of spousal maintenance, she can take a little time to decide what to do for employment. With Cosette away at college, she moves out. Heather moves in six weeks later.

Traveling is the only thing that feels right to Celia—to help her decide what to do with her life. Putting some furniture in storage, selling the rest, she hits the road. She's surprised that in spite of the massive fog of fright that sometimes rolls in, her upcoming adventure brings hope.

She allots two months for her travels, tallying her expenses in carefully penciled columns. In two months' time, she prays and hopes, she'll have a clue where she might want to live, what she might want to do for an income—to supplement monies made when her paintings are sold. She creates a loose itinerary with destinations in mind that might, somehow, feel like a place to make a new home. She considers Sedona, but it seems too touristy. She'll drive north to Prescott and Flagstaff, then to New Mexico. She thinks Santa Fe—maybe near the arts district, where she shows her paintings. Then Taos, north of Santa Fe, because she's seen pictures of those beautiful mountains and because it is a haven for artists and has a thriving spiritual community.

By the time she hits New Mexico, five weeks later, she's exhausted and frightened to the core. Nothing feels right. She's a drifter, a loner, a lost soul. Sleepless nights in motel rooms, greasy on-the-road meals, long hours behind the wheel. What was she thinking? She feels so lonely and so insignificant, she thinks she might disappear. Self-pity takes hold. *Why me?* Then, *it's all my fault,* run the old tapes in her head, when she thinks of Clay. *I should have done more of this, less of that,* she replays. She misses her house, she misses her life. In the depths of it, she wonders: *Would he have me back?*

It is soon after she has completely given up, fallen into a despair that resembles full surrender, hands up, weapons down, that she sees ahead, through a drizzle that smears her windshield (a crusty mix of dirt, dust and flattened bugs), the towering snow-capped Sangre de Cristo mountains piercing billowing clouds. Something calls to her. She laughs out loud. This is it. It isn't anything she can put into words. It feels like home. "Taos, New Mexico," she says aloud.

She drives slowly through town…a yoga studio, Mexican and Spanish restaurants, a ski shop, a health food store, an artists' cooperative, funky gift shops, art galleries, quaint hotels, two bookstores. Could she live here? Could this be home? She pulls into Hummingbird Lodge. An omen, she thinks. "You're one lucky lady," says the elderly gentleman seated behind the desk. "Had a cancellation call in this morning. It's a single—queen bed. You want it, it's yours."

Celia fiddles with the key, opens the door. She places her bag by the bed and stands still before the oval mirror atop the dresser. After a long journey, forty-two years long, she recognizes herself. She sees someone solid standing there. She can do this.

After a week at the hotel, Celia looks for a small place to rent. From a listing in the local paper, she comes upon a two-bedroom guest house on Penny and Mike Tigley's thick-with-trees, two-acre property. The Tigleys, retired, will be traveling throughout California for a few months or longer and want someone around, "just to keep an eye out," get the mail and water their many house plants. The rent is reasonable, the cottage is adorable, and Celia counts her blessings, a hundred times and more.

Two large suitcases and a travel bag; a box of books and tapes; a box of art supplies and folding easel; and two framed photos—one of Cosette and one of Paramahansa Yogananda—that's it. This shedding of many of her clothes, her furnishings, most of her accumulations and possessions, is freeing. She's surprised to find how little one really needs to get along. The day after she moves into her new place, she begins looking for a job. She's never had a "real" job—not painting pictures—in her entire life. The woman at the employment agency on Hickory Street studies her application, leans back in her chair, crosses her arms and says, "OK then, no skills, no typing, no computer, no retail, not even waiting tables. Tell me, Ms. Barrens, what *exactly* do you see yourself doing here?"

There's a "Help Wanted" sign at Bob Young's Nursery, but they want someone who can lift the large potted plants, bags of gravel and soil into the trucks. A secretarial job at Looton Manufacturing requires a minimum of two-years' experience with computers, a sales spot at a local radio station wants track record in sales or marketing. After six miserable days of cold calling—in boutiques, galleries, hotels, a photography shop, a tea house, a chiropractic office, and two spas, and filling out an application for a Target, soon to open, she curls up in bed, fully humiliated. *Should I go back to school? Take a computer class?* Celia is tired and decides to take a day off from "the hunt" to recharge. At this low point, she considers asking her mother for money, but sees it as a final humiliation and a tie that would falter a striving for true independence and unaided accomplishments.

The following morning—a brisk, clear Saturday, Celia takes her watercolor pad and watercolors to the mountains. Passing town, she sees the sign to the Taos Pueblo; she's driven by numerous times. She's intrigued by this Native American Indian Reservation, open to the public, but doesn't want to be one of the hordes of tourists who visit to view a culture America cruelly annihilated. In the distance, she can see the multi-storied adobe buildings. Of these earth-colored structures, one catches her eye—with a shiny aqua-painted door. That striking color combination is the lure as subject matter for a watercolor painting. She turns left into the parking lot. She walks the grounds of the adobe buildings, lingering at a shop selling intricately inlaid silver jewelry and painted pottery, peeks into a café, where a couple of sightseers sit at a table, both weary, eating fry bread, before she settles down to sketch, using charcoal to create her composition, then laying a watery wash of earth tones on her thick, grainy paper, adding contrast with the vivid door, and the full bloom of magenta bougainvillea on the structure's east-facing wall. The unpainted spaces on her paper, the bright white highlights on the rooftop and flowering plants, bring the picture to life. The building emanates a special energy. It's authentic, she concludes, not the "pueblo revival"—the faux adobe of the Southwestern architectural style she's seen throughout New Mexico. This structure is created of the earth, mixed with water and straw, and made into sun-dried bricks. A small sign says they were constructed between 1000 and 1450 AD, making them the oldest continuously inhabited dwellings in the country. Celia thinks it's amazing to see and paint a place that despite all attempts to destroy it and its culture, has survived. The sign relates that 150 people still make this pueblo their home—descendants of those who created the village over 1,000 years ago.

Lost in concentration, she doesn't see a man standing near her, watching her paint. He's tall and broad, his long black hair blowing in the breeze, wearing a worn jean jacket. He smiles at her and says, "You see." Celia isn't sure what he means, how to respond. Her expression shows her uncertainty and he clarifies: "It is with reverence that you draw and paint. You honor this home, my home. You see. You see it as a symbol of Indian resistance to external rule. Blessings upon you."

"Oh, my." Celia mutters, flattered and embarrassed. "Thank you, really, for saying that. If you'd like, well, only if…would you like to have the picture? It's your home…can I give it to you as a gift?"

"I would be honored," he says.

His name is Deryle Cordova. He has lived at Taos Pueblo all his life. His father and uncle are potters and silversmiths, who also live on the reservation.

A slender, pretty woman with black hair cascading to her waist, wearing a bright red sweater and white jeans, opens the shiny turquoise door. Two little girls, giggling, one carrying a jump rope, dart out. Deryle shows his wife, Rose, the picture, which she studies, standing there in the walkway for eternity, Celia thinks. Then, she looks up at Celia, tears in her glossy brown eyes and hugs her. She insists that Celia come in, have something to eat. The house is sunny and smells of vanilla and cinnamon. The furnishings are few, but elegant. Coloring books and crayons, and sippy cups litter the kitchen table, where they sit, eating just-baked oatmeal cookies, warm, thick and lumpy with raisins, and sipping ice-cold milk. They sit and speak, as if old friends, for over an hour—of marriage and children, of art and travel. Rose is the second grade teacher at the pueblo's elementary school and they're looking for an art teacher, she tells Celia. The pay "isn't great," Rose says, but it comes with benefits—health insurance—and you have the summers off. Celia feels a tingling all the way to her toes, but then sinks. "Don't I need a master's?" she says. "I only have a bachelors."

"You can get hired on a waiver and then take the grad school credits to qualify. It's actually how I did it, when I started. It's tough to fill these teaching spots—because the pay's low. New Mexico needs teachers."

Chapter Twenty-Six

REINVENTION

AFTER A HARROWING COUPLE OF WEEKS trying to learn 60 kids' names, pretending she knew what on earth she was doing, and developing, to save her life, a tough-teacher stance that required an occasional bellowing holler, threats of visits to the principal and letters sent home, Celia was off to a decent start. By November, she's in a groove and starts to love her work. The creative energy of her kids fuels her. There are her favorites—Wanda and Sharon, the twins in fourth grade, who have real talent; Alan, the shy, new boy, who loves to draw; and then, the troublemakers—Danny Winter and J.T. Yazzie, who she might murder. Wednesday nights are allotted to the first of her graduate school classes, with plans to complete the remaining requirements over two consecutive summers. Paradoxically, she is both exhausted and exhilarated, feeling weary by day's end, but also fulfilled by the busy life she now leads, a life she can rightly claim as her own.

Two snowy Christmases come and go, Cosette alternating holidays and summers with her parents. Celia racks up all of her graduate credits over evening classes and a busy summer. It's at her graduation dinner with Tim and Maria and her son Arlo—friends of Celia's from school, and Rose and Deryle and their daughters, at Tim's Stray Dog Cantina, that Celia runs into the parents of one of Cosette's former schoolmates—Robin and Jack Cartoff, vacationing in Taos. Robin stands at Celia's table, her hand at her heart, and says, "I can't believe it—is that you Celia? Celia Barrens?" It isn't so much Celia's short hair (a chic do she cut the previous spring), or the big silver and turquoise earrings dangling to her chin (a graduation gift from Rose and Deryle), that alter her appearance, it's her whole persona that's changed. Her body movements are languid, her face relaxed, her complexion rosy, her eyes clear and sparkly. She is happy.

. . .

It is on a Friday afternoon, a bitter cold December day of the following school year, when sleet had turned to snow, soon after the students have gone home, that Celia encounters an odd visitor to her classroom. He's seen her at the teacher pancake breakfasts and the art fairs, he says. He has a powerful presence and, although the door is open and she hears some kids and Mr. Brackus, the gym teacher, in the hall, she feels nervous. He perceives this and says, "No worries, no reason to fear. We have not yet met...I am Wanda and Sharon's grandfather. They call me Baba," he smiles here at the recollection of this endearment, "but my name is Raymond Redhorse, although most people call me Ray. I am here to help you."

Celia sets down the jars of paint she's been stacking and gives him a wary look. "Help how?" she says, moving toward the door, pretending to straighten some books on a shelf there. This man unsettles her.

"It is about your spirit, your soul."

"Excuse me?" she says, surprising herself, hearing her own harsh inflection.

"There is no need to oppose me. I assure you," he says, slightly bowing his head, his graying hair in a long, neat braid, swung over his shoulder, revealing ears studded with small multi-colored jewels. He wears a bright blue ski jacket and a thick, hand-knit scarf of burgundy, black and blue, heavily fringed. His face is lined in deep grooves. "Perhaps I have approached you too suddenly. Forgive me. I don't know how to share what I know with you."

Celia tries to remain calm. "And what is it that you know?"

"That you do not embody your full presence. This is how I can help. I bring pieces of your soul back to you. How can I say this without offending you? I am aware of a piece of your soul that wants to go home, back to you." Celia laughs. It is a strange response…a reaction of fear, of weariness, of pure release. Ray laughs, too.

They sit quietly after the tension breaks, Celia considering him. His eyes, deep brown, are kind and knowing. When he sees that she's relaxed, that she finally is open to him, he offers, "It is not hard to do, but of course, it takes your belief, your cooperation. You can 'think on it,' as they say." He smiles here. "Talk to Rose. I know you trust her and I have worked with her and her family. Just let me know. I offer you this gift because of what you give my grandchildren." And with that, Ray walks out the door and slowly down the hall.

. . .

"Ray Redhorse—he's what you'd call a shaman," says Rose, wiping off the chalkboard, lining up the erasers on the ledge. Celia is relieved to find that Rose hasn't left school yet, eager to evaluate her strange encounter. An image of a shaman flashes in Celia's head: a man wearing a headdress, hopping on one foot, chanting something nonsensical, tapping his palm on his open mouth. She's embarrassed by these stereotypical ideas she has.

"I love Ray. Everyone loves Ray. He's what you might call our holy man. He helps our community in many ways…healing the sick, shifting the weather, guiding spirits to the dead. He helped my mom's sister to her resting place," says Rose, gathering papers stacked on her desk, sliding them into her knapsack. "When Audrey was sick last year—she was missing a lot of school—he gave her herbs. Really helped. Hasn't been sick since."

"How did he become a shaman? I mean, is it something he learned, or, well, how does he know what to do?"

"His father was a holy man, here, too, before he passed—about ten years ago. Some of what Ray knows comes from his dad, but most shamans obtain their powers from what some might call a dark night of the soul. It can be a physical illness that takes someone for a loop, or sometimes an emotional or psychic breakdown. It's through this kind of crisis that strength and resilience is summoned. It's hard to describe…but through a certain level of loss and pain, the ego is let go and a spiritual knowingness comes through. With Ray, he almost lost his life in a motorcycle accident."

"He said he'd like to help me integrate my spirit or something like that, bring back a part of my soul."

Rose looks up, swings her backpack over her shoulder and smiles. "Oh Celia, you should work with him, really. It's more common than you think—soul loss comes from an illness or sometimes trauma. It's like pieces of yourself fragment, kind of fly off—this affects your life force. A shaman sees these soul retrievals as resolution for the whole community—not just the individual. Ray connects with spirits, through prayer and ritual. He's like, well, an intermediary between the natural and the supernatural. I know you're open to this kind of thing, but it probably sounds crazy to you."

"Nothing seems crazy anymore, Rosie."

…

The drumming reminds Celia of her work with Adelair and animal totems. Ray stands by the window, slowly beating a handheld drum, facing a cluster of tall trees, as Celia gets on her back atop a chief's blanket that Ray placed on the floor in her living room. She can see, beyond him, the morning's first light color the sky a golden hue. He suggested that they meet at dawn. She lets the steady rhythm of the drum soothe her. He's brought with him many treasures, placed around her at the edges of a thick, wool blanket underneath her, patterned with geometric shapes of red, black and brown. There are eagle feathers, a handmade flute, a tattered cloth—its beading almost worn off, several smooth black stones, the shed skin of a snake, and an elaborately carved rattle with feathers dangling from its handle.

His drumming slows and as the sound fades, he begins to sing. His voice is deep and sorrowful, almost pleading, a moan. It's a language she does not know. The sad, but beautiful sound reaches deep into her heart and tears pour forth. "This is the song of your soul," he says to her. "If you wish, you may follow it."

Her eyes closed, Celia sees herself in a cave. Her children, two daughters—their ages maybe six and eight—are wrapped in her arms. Her husband sits across from his family, gazing at her with loving eyes. They're chanting...chanting the same song that Ray sings. In this vision, she and her husband know that their deaths are imminent...the enemy, the white men, are upon them and they will be scalped. She is filled with terror and desperately trying to be strong, trying to continue singing, to continue singing the song. The pain of losing her children, of having them harmed, is excruciating. The song is what she holds onto to maintain her courage for the sake of her daughters.

Then, she is high above the cave, in the sky, flying in the sky. She is a bird, soaring high, swooping low, in complete control. She is free, floating, joyous, all-knowing.

After several minutes of silence, Ray says, "A full moon lights the night sky. You are 14-months-old. This is the moment of fragmentation, an escape you made so that you could live. At the instant when you could have chosen death, you chose life, yet a piece of you parted—your discrimination, your knowingness—and now we welcome it home." Next, he circles Celia with the rattle, shaking it vigorously. It is loud, very loud, and she feels it shaking things up, somehow shaking up her thought patterns, the constructs in her head. Then, he kneels over her, places his hand on her abdomen. His hand gives off heat that seems to open her up. "There, we have placed it back with you. First, it takes root like a tree, enabling your nourishment from Mother Earth. Your roots will grow deep. When a storm brews, when winds reach great speed, you will sway, not snap. From here forward, as lesser lights descend, as darkness engulfs, you will possess keen judgment, encompassing knowledge of your circumstance, appraisal of your surroundings. On this auspicious day, your ancestors rejoice. Behold their smiles."

Celia is crying so hard, she's shaking, almost convulsing, lacking the ability to hold anything back. The emotional release is enormous—a flood gate has swung open after a decades-long dam.

"Your trust will grow with time," Ray continues. "This is your goal if you so choose it. You can have love, earthly love. Look toward a man you feel at peace with. He has a heart of gold, wisdom of the ages, softness of a breeze, gentleness of a swallow."

Ray begins to hum an odd, folksy song, and then quiets to say, "Mother Earth speaks to us." Circling Celia in measured steps, his quiet, rhythmic voice descends and replenishes like gentle rain. To Celia, it sounds like a poem: "You will witness the crumbling of the old to institute the new. The hierarchy dismantles, so love and joy can be infused. Old ways must make way for the new. Help your fellow man especially if he falls; community is all. Love with all of your heart. Give back. Reciprocity is all. Love takes hold. Love reigns. Love rules. The outcome is assured. The dark and greed subside, assisted by the light of womankind. The dark ages are through. Love conquers all, the way it should."

Ray touches the top of Celia's head with his palm, which she intuits as a signal that the healing has come to a close. Her lids are heavy; they feel locked shut. When she opens her eyes, the room slowly comes into focus. Ray is seated cross-legged, his hands in prayer at his chest, his head bowed in reverence toward the window. Eagle feathers have been placed at her feet. Too hard to keep her eyes open, too hard to keep awake…she drifts off into sleep. As she sleeps, entering dreamtime to integrate her soul retrieval, Ray sits quietly in meditation, offering gratitude to Mother Earth, to his ancestors, and to his guides.

Trumpets sound. A flock of over 100,000 white doves released from the heavens, flapping their wings in unison, fly down, descending further still to the doorstep of every seeker of love and light on the planet Earth and leave a white feather as a prophecy of love and joy to come.

When Celia wakes, Ray rises, walks to her and pulls a small leather pouch from his pocket. "This is corn meal," he says, instructing Celia to sprinkle it outside near a favorite tree or plant to give the Earth a gift in return for her healing.

Celia sees Ray to the front door and watches him walk down the narrow brick path, then kneel to pick up something. He pivots and raises a long white feather, which he gives to Celia with a wide smile and a small bow.

Celia scribbles as much as she can remember into her journal. Her skepticism never seems to quit as she wonders if her otherworldly healing experience could actually enact an effect. *Could a piece of my soul split off? Could Ray actually call it back? Did I have a previous life as a Native American woman, who lost her life and her family to such a vicious attack? What kind of downfall is in store? How will love rule the world?*

And what was all that about Mr. Right? Sure...a guy as gentle as a swallow. Hmph. Wary of romantic love—the stuff of pop songs and good guys in movies and books, she muses. Celia feels no readiness to enter into a new relationship. She feels so raw, so vulnerable, hesitant to let anyone into her heart. She has summoned everything she has to build her core, to be strong. She's fearful of letting anyone in who might discourage her.

Chapter Twenty-Seven

BREATHE

INITIALLY, THE CHANGES ARE SUBTLE. Whereas most things in recent years lined up for Celia, almost suddenly an opposite pattern takes hold. Budget cuts at the elementary school result in a dearth of art supplies. In response, she fills her classroom's art closet with paints, brushes, modeling clay, paper and markers purchased with her paltry paycheck. Money is pretty tight on her salary. Then, her trusty car craps out one afternoon in the school parking lot. The repairs: $1,400. The following month, her landlords timidly approach her with the bad news: They've sold the house and are moving to California. The new owners will take possession in two months—she'll have to be out. They're terribly sorry. She's been a wonderful tenant, blah, blah, blah. She's starting to get really pissed off. When Jeremy, the new second grader, drops a hefty box of clay on her right foot and it breaks two bones requiring a cast to her knee and a set of crutches, she's had enough. When she learns that surgery is required for pins, she is starting to get seriously fed up. But, just weeks later, the big clunker: Most music and art programs throughout the state will be slashed—huge cuts. They'll completely cut art from her school. On June 10th, she'll be out of work.

She tries summoning her saints, her angels, to no regard. Nothing. No help. Are they blind to her plight? She's furious and also scared. *How could this be happening,* she wonders, *after all the work I've done on myself? Did I come this far to get a cosmic kick in the butt? Have I done something wrong? Is this a punishment?* Fear takes root. She thinks she's banished this ugly, unwanted houseguest, but he's back, unpacking a large, rolling suitcase—no overnight bag slung over his shoulder.

She finds Ray by the cluster of cottonwood trees by the lake—a place he often visits, and pleads for help: "What's going on?" He looks at her with deep reverence and compassion. "Please, please, tell me what to do. Everything's falling apart."

"Celia, dear, first let's breathe and then we'll sit and talk."

They sit on the wood benches in the tall grasses at the east end of the lake, face to face. He asks her to follow, to imitate, his breath—a slow, deep inhalation, then holding, then a release. They sit and breathe like this for a few minutes, then he speaks…

"This is your initiation, but I know, it seems treacherous. It is your contract, so to speak, in this lifetime to relinquish your earthly attachments, to enter the realm of the spiritual. It is a document, in a sense, that you have signed. The timing is now—for the losses that descend upon you at this hour are soon to come for much of humankind, resulting from greed and disrespect for Mother Earth. In this world, the divine feminine has been lost and is in dire need of resurrection." Here, Ray closes his eyes and looks heavenward.

"You will walk through it. By your own example, and the examples of numerous lightworkers, others will see the door. It is that simple. The door is always ajar. Each and every time a soul endures hardship and makes it through, an energetic gridwork of light is set, a template, so to speak, for others to latch onto. It is probably difficult for you to fathom, but you willingly chose this path that you find yourself on. Nothing is being done to you, as you imagine. Like a small plant turning towards the sun, you are following the light, leading to source, going home. This knowledge that I impart provides something to hold onto. See it as a gift. It is hard now to feel grateful, I know, I've been through it, but you are blessed to have this understanding, for it will hold you up when you think you might sink, when you want to give up." Ray lifts his arms high, his palms to the sky, then closes them in prayer at his heart.

Grateful? Ha. Celia feels nothing close to gratitude. She's incensed. *If I've taken on this truckload of trouble by my own choosing, then I'm an idiot, a fool. What was I thinking? I've been through enough. Enough is enough. I need a new contract. I need a good lawyer.*

Chapter Twenty-Eight

SELF-PITY ENTERS STAGE LEFT

THE NEWSPAPER REPORTS THE HOTTEST July in 22 years, a seemingly endless stretch of high-nineties and humid. Twice, there are blackouts due to energy over-usage. Celia runs her floor fan on high, skimping on air conditioning to cover the rent in her new apartment—a cheap, icky one bedroom on Massey Street, near the railroad tracks. Propped on pillows, her foot and leg throb. The painkillers she took after the surgery shut down her digestive tract like a ten-car pileup, so she figured she'd endure the pain, which she lessens, somewhat, by too much Ibuprofen and an herbal tincture from Ray that numbs her brain, more than anything. Her mother generously offered money, but Celia declined. It's temporary poverty, she rationalized. Her dignity was already on a thread. Taking a check from her mother would have cut her down to nothing.

She tries to be hopeful, but her grief has many players. On different days, a variety of characters take center stage. Humiliation shows up frequently and he's pretty menacing. His forte is comparing her to other people—women her age, women who are married, have careers, homes (mortgages almost paid down), and both working legs. Self-pity enters stage left, a little fellow with scrawny arms and legs and a pinched face, who looks like a bug. He shuffles around with a pathetic song and dance number—a woe-is-me tune—and is booed off stage, dodging overripe tomatoes. Remorse, with his twin brother Regret, have their tiresome, worn-out dialog that Celia is weary of hearing. Their act leaves her feeling that everything bad that's happened is all her fault. This is when she hobbles to the kitchen, irresponsibly forgoing her crutches, for that jar of chunky peanut butter and crackers, even though she's putting on weight. Hitting forty-five seems to have not simply slowed down her metabolism, but shut it off. Recently, she joined the largest club of women: the calorie counters.

Fear is her constant companion, her bedfellow…fear of running down her savings before she's well, fear of sliding further down the chute. Heeelp! Who knows what's next—what bad news might befall her when she answers the ominously ringing telephone or opens the letter with no return address. *Dear Ms. Barrens: This is to inform you that you are being pushed to the breaking point for no apparent reason. There is no destiny, no God, just random evil.* Her movements become measured and small, like an animal threatened in the jungle. Her instinct is to cower, to freeze, to avoid being dinner.

One week post-surgery, with more of her strength restored, she puts up the good fight…clipping grocery coupons, straightening up the apartment, taking vitamins, tossing the glazed doughnuts and half-devoured chocolate bunny (a gift from a student) in the garbage, completing and sending job applications to other school districts. With so many programs cut throughout the state, art teachers glut the market. Teaching spots in the arts are almost non-existent, so she's thrilled to land a spot at an elementary school in Redmond, two hours northwest, near the famed Four Corners— where New Mexico reaches Arizona, Utah and Colorado. Can she begin on August 25—a week before the first day of school? That gives her 17 days, total, to move. Yikes. "Yes, yes, of course I can." After a Friday afternoon touring the school with Mr. Sparks, the assistant principal, and finding a small two-bedroom the following day, which does have a lot of light and a view of a park, she packs her things and moves north. She hopes to relish a rush of relief, bask in a celebratory mindset for securing a new job, but when she pulls in front of her new home and cuts the ignition, something doesn't feel right. That "something" will soon be disclosed.

. . .

Those first few months in Redmond would have registered *tilt* in a game of pinball. Packing and unpacking too soon after surgery, reorienting to new surroundings, beginning a new job...dizzying and exhausting. When her health takes a slide, she chalks it up to the culprit of modern-day living: stress and overtired. And there's something sort of, well, depressing about her new position. The school building is old and ugly. She thinks it's narrow for this to bother her, but it does. And the administrators are disorganized, the teachers unfriendly and harried. She likes the kids, but it's daunting establishing her authority and rapport with them.

Her ailments increase: Headaches, at first, then fatigue, muscle aches, hair loss, interrupted sleep, followed by a rash on her torso and palms, digestive troubles and spots in front of her eyes. She's scared. She has blood tests. All numbers come in within range.

It's Jim Saunders, the sixth grade teacher, who clues her in. He's the only person who's made her feel welcome in her new job—stopping by her classroom that first week, introducing himself, "Holler if you need anything," motioning that his classroom was across the hall. One day after school, when he comes by to say hi, she opens up and tells him about her health problems. "You're probably more sensitive than most," he says. "The plants are just 15 miles northwest. Not that far for the wind to carry the ash. And, you know, there's the whole controversy with the ground water."

Every muscle in Celia's body freezes. *What? What in the world is he talking about?*

"You know—the San Juan Generating Station." Celia had heard of that. "One of the largest coal-fired power plants in the country," he says. Terror envelopes her, as he continues. "Underneath the desert here are billions of tons of low-sulfur coal. Add the water provided by the San Juan River and seriously poor, desperate-to-find-work folks, and you're sitting on the perfect place for a power plant. The Four Corners Plant was built on the south side of the San Juan River in '63; the San Juan Generating Station went up 10 years later, on the north side. By the mid-seventies, they were spewing thousands of tons of poisonous particles, but with new air quality laws and regional activism, the plants were forced to comply—putting in pollution control devices. OK, then, you think—great. But, here's the rub: Every single pound of pollution kept out of the air winds up in solid waste. The pollution control devices only made the problem on the ground worse. You hear what I'm saying?" Celia nods, gesturing for Jim to take a seat, as she almost falls into hers.

"It's called flyash—the solid waste—piled up like a mountain at the plant, where it blows around or leaches into the ground," Jim continues, sitting down, reaching for his necktie, pulling it loose. "You should drive out there, take a look. You won't believe it—I tell you…you won't believe your eyes. *Huge*—some 25-million tons of crap. Another 50-million tons has been dumped in a nearby mine. From there, it can seep into the water table, migrating to drinking water supplies. I'm talking lead, mercury and arsenic. Folks started getting sick, real sick. There were lawsuits; there were settlements, but no directive to clean it up."

"Why?" asks Celia, incredulously.

"Because there's nothing, zip, zero, that violates either state or national guidelines. You ready for this? The EPA, the Environmental Protection Agency, doesn't even treat it as hazardous waste. It's classified under the rules for non-municipal, non-hazardous waste, which throws it into a hodgepodge of rules and regulations that differ from state to state." I've been poisoned, Celia thinks. "You OK?" Jim asks. "You're looking mighty pale. Probably scaring the bejesus out of you. You want a glass a water?" He jumps ups and walks to the sink. The last thing in the whole world she wants is a drink from that sink.

"No, no, thanks…what…I mean—why didn't anyone say anything to me when I applied for the job?"

"Yeah—right. I can hear it now: *Well, Ms. Barrens, you're perfectly qualified, but are you aware of the highly toxic dumpsite nearby?* That's not the world *I'm* living in. We're far enough away here in Redmond to pretend it doesn't exist. It's mostly the folks living nearer to the plants that are symptomatic. Get a load of this: Studies were just published showing that the ozone levels there are nowhere near EPA standards. Most Redmond folks want to deny it—you know, real estate values and all that. Hey—it's the American way—head in the sand, not my backyard."

Jim looks up at the wall clock and says he has to run. As he opens the door, he turns and says, "There's a little storefront down the street from the post office…Coalition for Change or something. You'll see it. Andy Mack's the guy you want to see. He knows everything about it." His expression is sad and apologetic. The door slowly shuts behind him.

Celia is frightened and furious. She wants to leave, leave that afternoon. Get in her car and drive. Drive away, as far away as possible. But, she grabs her backpack and drives straight toward the post office—to find out more, to find out what to do.

. . .

Andy Mack sits behind a dented steel desk piled with papers. He's deep in thought when Celia enters, glancing up from his laptop, offering a distracted smile. The office is tiny and messy and littered with cardboard boxes, the windows smudged and yellowed. Central casting has selected him for activist—20-something, scruffy beard, T-shirt blaring "Coal Ash: Profit for Industry. Poison for People," handsome, but unkempt, because the precarious position of the planet is a higher priority than taking a bath. His bicycle leans against the back wall—an old blue racing bike with a sun-bleached helmet hanging from the handlebars. A rack on the back holds a battered green nylon backpack.

"Hey, I'm Andy," he offers, pushing back his squeaky chair, now focusing his gaze fully on Celia, who has no idea where to begin after introducing herself, but manages to narrate some largely incoherent story about her health and her recent employment. His eyes are soft and kind. "I know this is hard. I can help," he says.

Quickly rising to clear off a chair, he gestures for Celia to take the seat. He gathers some pamphlets and begins saying things she doesn't want to hear. He addresses her health first: "Mercury is likely high…you should get your level checked. It's in both the air and the water. Northern New Mexico has one of the highest airborne levels in the country—from the smoke spewed from the coal plants," he tells her. "Coal plants are responsible for roughly 98% of utility-related mercury pollution," he continues, "and are the single largest source of mercury emissions in the country. Mercury toxicity could cause *all* your health problems."

But there are all kinds of other toxins, too, he says, 67 different ones from the plant, with names she's never heard of—that he describes as neurotoxins, cardiopulmonary irritants and carcinogens, which are now a part of her world. A report just surfaced, he says, intentionally kept secret by the government, showing cancer risks, as well as damage to liver, kidney and the nervous system from drinking water polluted by coal ash. Children and the elderly are most susceptible, but also anyone with a compromised immune system. Outraged, Celia thinks of her students. Her thoughts turn fast to her broken foot, recent surgery, loss of her job, the frantic move, the new job—her immune system was already on overload.

"Aidan Pierce—he's the guy you want to see—a local doc, but into alternative healing. He'll test your mercury levels and tell you about detoxing. Here's his card—he's nearby on Arroyo Avenue. Here's my card and some pamphlets with pertinent info—and a list of ways to get involved."

Living nightmare, is her first thought, as she walks up the block in a daze to her car, passing the post office, where an American flag flaps in the breeze. She feels a raging fury for the ways in which the government and corporate greed are sickening people, children!, stealing their most precious asset—their health. Fear envelopes her…will she survive this? She'll have to quit her job, move once more. She's already so worn out. She wants to curl up somewhere and give up, but she recalls and relies on Ray's encouraging words for strength and calls Dr. Pierce when she gets home. The next available appointment is the following afternoon at 4:30. That night, she can't sleep.

Dr. Pierce has office hours three days a week. On Mondays and Tuesdays he pays house calls to children who can't afford healthcare on Indian reservations throughout the region. Tall and thin, his curly brown hair wild, wearing a faded denim shirt with a striped tie, he explains that he trained traditionally at Johns Hopkins, but gave up on most Western modes of healing years ago. Celia feels open to his philosophy—having grown increasingly distrustful of some doctors, who prescribe pills with side effects and send you home, often treating symptoms, not the root cause.

When she's diagnosed with elevated mercury levels, he offers options that might enable her to stay in Redmond: an air purifier for her home and classroom, only bottled water—even for cooking, filters on her shower, and a detoxification protocol. Her decision comes readily, as the whole environment begins to haunt her. She quits her job and heads back to Arizona. She'll follow Dr. Pierce's detox protocol there, away from the poison water and air. He assures her she'll recover, but it'll take time—a year to fully regain her health. She rents a room in a widow's house in Sedona advertised on the Internet. *Temporary*, she tells herself. The day after she unpacks, she falls into the mother of all depressions. She reaches out to Dr. Kerrigan Holme for help. She needs an old friend, a healer, a mother-figure.

...

It had been 17 years. Celia hugs Kerrigan and starts to cry. When she calms down enough to fully elaborate on her plight, Kerrigan assures her that clarity about her circumstance will be revealed on the massage table and encourages her to begin her session. Having progressed on her spiritual path, Kerrigan is even more adept at channeling her guides during sessions, relating their messages to her clients.

"You must possess nothing in order to be given everything," Kerrigan commences, her hands hovering above Celia's legs. "Your courage on your spiritual path has led you to this final lesson. You will attempt grabbing onto the last vestiges; it is human nature. But your goal is to transcend, to release everything you have relied on, so that you may relinquish the ego, enabling the loss of fear. When your grief transcends all bounds, you will arrive. Nothing to lose is the optimal state. The gate to paradise is often entered through your deepest pain. This is the greatest riddle. When all the effort you can muster reaches nowhere, you will break free. Like a caged bird, you will finally fly free, and looking back, see that you were the cage and the key. Your personal arrogance tumbles; your defense mechanisms falter. Once humbled, emptied and purified, you become the light of love and a beacon for others."

Kerrigan's hands lightly touching Celia's forehead, she continues in a soft voice: "Here, I am energizing your cells, but certain medical issues require specific protocols. Follow the prescribed regimen of the generous doctor. He knows the body and how to rid it of toxins. Much illness in our time is a result of our polluted environment. Your healing will be long and arduous, but your success is assured if you adhere to his program. He is a divine being incarnate, one who will help heal the people and the land, for the Earth is ill, its resources plundered, its plight a sorry reflection of mass disrespect and disregard. Mother Earth is the great nurturer, yet people have stolen her wealth, attempted to usurp her power." Celia takes hold of Kerrigan's words as if drowning, clinging to a sole piece of driftwood in a turbulent sea. With Kerrigan's fingers gently touching her temples, Celia drifts into a deep, restorative sleep.

Chapter Twenty-Nine

SURRENDER

HOLED UP IN HER TINY RENTED ROOM in Sedona, this metamorphosis Celia hopes to undergo doesn't feel exactly sacred; it feels more like eating crow. The ego requires quite the beating to wear itself out, to finally let go. She feels less a spiritually evolved soul and more like a two-year old splayed on the floor, kicking and wailing. Going down isn't easy. For the first time in many years, she considers ending it all, taking her life. It's a fleeting thought, overcome by her steadfast belief in reincarnation and her conclusion that all she'll get is a rain check. She has to do her work, this lifetime or the next. There's no escape, no exit.

Surrender comes in stages. First, she makes up her mind that if her vanity will be ground down to powder, her pride burnt to ash, she'll attempt it with grace. At Kerrigan's directive, she dedicates herself to regaining her health by following Dr. Pierce's protocol, pulling the heavy metal from her body in stages, as he instructed, using herbs and seaweeds, and other chelation protocols. Vitamins and minerals, a specialized diet, colonics, saunas, moderate exercise and breathwork also play a part. This healing regimen seems a full-time job. When she isn't putting hours into healing, she gives time to Coalition for Change as a volunteer—seeking grant monies by filing applications on the Internet. In this way, her fury is aimed at a cause. Coalition for Change, she learns, uses its funds to lobby for changes in energy consumption to help stop the country's reliance on coal. Andy Mack aims to enact a moratorium on the construction of new coal-fired power plants in the Southwest and ultimately phase out coal altogether, employing sun and wind as energy sources. In the interim, he hopes to help place caps on carbon emissions and enact legislation for the storage and disposal of coal ash.

While most days she feels brave, like a spiritual warrior, occasionally she falls apart, losing all confidence in God's game plan, as she thinks of it. Fear rises up and takes hold—grabs her by the neck and won't let go. It's hardly constructive, but she plays and replays a mental list of her losses. The loss of her marriage, home, and child head her list of absent inventory. This last one—her child—is a big exaggeration, for Cosette has simply gone off to college and is now in graduate school, but to Celia it feels like a loss just the same, and besides, she's into flagrant self-pitying. She's been marketed this package of home, husband, and family by every conceivable means and to wind up without it feels like a big, fat "F". Her health, of course, is paramount and now gone. Her job—gone. Her youth is over, she feels, and this current state of affairs is not quite the way she pictured approaching the milestone of fifty—just two years off. She's pared down her belongings and is living like a monk, yet she sometimes longs for the goodies of materialism. Screw asceticism, she thinks. As a seemingly final blow, her hair has fallen out in clumps. This is something serious, not a few more hairs in the brush. Dr. Pierce has assured her it will grow back. She worries; she doubts.

As usual, only out of utter desperation does she hunker down and meditate more. She's reminded of Joelle Kimpter, one of her kindergarteners, who sulked and said, "I don't want to go," when they boarded the bus for a school trip to the county museum and then, announced on the way back, "It was the best day ever," grinning ear to ear. After all these years, Celia still bucks, still resists. *Why is that?* For time and time again, her meditation practice is the perfect antidote to her fear. Her connection with higher entities always infuses her with hope and love.

So, twice a day, first thing in the morning and just before bed, she meditates. She does this for many months until the anticipated surrender manifests, releasing her fear, replacing it with peace. Her insistence on control is at last relinquished; her surrender is complete. With the many roles in which she sees herself stripped away (doting mother, good wife, hard-working artist and teacher, healthy citizen), and only the essence of herself—her soul—remaining, her identification aligns with her unbreakable core, the authentic part of herself. All the defeat that she has endured dismantles her ego. The other shoe has already dropped. The worst has already taken place. All already lost, fear of loss is finally purposeless and expendable. It is wholly freeing. "When you ain't got nothing, you got nothing to lose," she hears Bob Dylan crooning on her car radio.

After this deeply felt shift in her consciousness, following a long meditation one evening, she drifts into a sound sleep and a vivid dream— the most disturbing dream she's ever had. This is how it began: She's knocking on the door to an old house—a large Victorian in need of painting and repairs. When no one answers, she ventures inside to find a group of women sitting around a table wearing long black dresses and white cotton caps with ruffled brims, tied beneath their chins. They work diligently, picking seeds from clusters of dried leaves, chatting about the healing properties of varied remedies they're making for market and for their families. They speak of belladonna and goldenseal. One of the women looks frightened, hearing footsteps. Suddenly, several uniformed men, having broken into the house through the backdoor, march in, seize the women and their herbs, yelling something about locking them in jail.

The dream continues…Celia runs into an adjoining room to escape. It's a small bedroom. Behind the canopied bed strewn with sheer lace, where she hides, she can see through an opening on the side…a soldier grabs a young girl by her long hair, yanks her down. He unzips his pants, forces her. The woman is screaming, fighting him, but he's twice her size and soon, she succumbs, looking out to Celia, helpless, scared, meeting her eyes. Celia tries to scream for help, but nothing comes out. She reaches to grab a tall candlestick to hit the soldier, but she grabs at nothing, at thin air.

Celia runs…runs down the hall and through an open door. There, she sees row after row of young girls, seated close at tables, cutting cloth, stitching seams on antiquated sewing machines, pressing seams with steaming irons. It is so hot, Celia can hardly breathe. She searches for a window, but there is none. She tries opening a door, but it's locked. She bangs and finally bursts through, entering a large room…a courtroom and she takes a seat in the back. The benches are lined with women, each on trial for an offense. One by one, they rise, walk to the front, announce their crime to the judge and jury. Some seem ashamed, their faces cast low; others lift their chins high, their eyes ablaze with defiance. Celia listens to their unlawful acts: distributing information on birth control, teaching girls to read and write, wearing trousers, not wearing a headscarf, collecting signatures, convening meetings, stepping forward as a rape victim, sheltering a neighbor from abuse, refusing an arranged marriage, opposing the loss of her home and property. Engrossed and appalled, Celia does not hear the police officer approach her from behind. He grabs her wrist and drags her to the front of the room, shoves her to the front of the line, where she's instructed to recite her crime. She searches her mind, frantically…*what have I done wrong? What is my act against the law?* She hears herself say, "I am a witch," and the judge sternly retorts, "To be burned alive."

And at this revelation, she wakes, drenched in sweat, shaking. She sits at the bed's edge trying to slow her breath. When she calms down, she doesn't know what to make of this dream. *Is it a retracing, throughout history, of the oppression of women? Is there a message for me in the last part about a witch? Is it a clue to a past life?* She thinks to call Ray Redhorse for advice. He answers the phone on the first ring and before she utters one word, says, "Ah, Celia. Wonderful. I've been thinking of you."

She's astonished at his psychic power. "That's amazing," she replies. "You knew it was me."

Ray chuckles and says, "I have caller ID." Celia laughs, too.

After hearing the recent events in her life and listening to her dream, Ray encourages Celia to enact a ritual that will provide understanding. He advises that she visit a favorite spot—ideally outside, surrounded by nature. By following his instructions, he says, she can access this possible past life on her own. She's hesitant. If she really was accused of witchcraft and brought to trial in a past life, does she want to re-experience it? She wonders if she might somehow get stuck in the past. Is that possible? When Celia shares her concerns with Ray, he responds nonchalantly: "What happens is what happens." This is not exactly all that encouraging.

Yet, that afternoon, she drives to Sedona's Boynton Canyon and follows Ray's initial instruction to "set up the energies," which is almost identical to the way her meditation tapes begin. She sits crossed-legged beneath the shade of a tree and pulls into her body the energies from the Earth (from the Earth's core, as well as the mountains surrounding her), then, resonates with these powerful, yet peaceful frequencies and feels them fill her heart. Then, she spirals them up to her head, then melds them with high energies descending from above. Next, she's been instructed to imagine a long tunnel and at its end a door. Supposedly, when she walks through this imaginary door, she'll see herself as someone else—as her soul reincarnated in a past life. "It may feel like your imagination," Ray said, "but, follow it all the same." So, as Celia opens this make-believe door, she thinks just that— I'm making this up. Yet, the specificity of the costume of the woman she finds seated there seems beyond Celia's knowledge. The woman wears a long dress, fitted in the bodice, made of brown cotton with maroon velvet trimming the hem and pleated bloussant sleeves. The neckline is high and lacey. Beaded necklaces hang low across her chest. A flat cap, also of brown fabric, sits atop her head. Her wrists are adorned with bangles; on her fingers she wears many rings. Her face is pale, her expression serious. Her presence is so real, so palpable, Celia feels she could touch her. In this vision, she's seated among two others—a husband and wife, in their opulent home. The wife's face is cast down, ashamed of her husband's scorn. Celia intuits that the husband has accused Celia of casting a spell, culminating in the stillbirth of their son. Celia was a midwife—assisting women through pregnancy and childbirth—and midwives were in danger of becoming scapegoats for complications in pregnancy and childbirth as the witch craze swept through their town, a small village in Germany.

Ray's instruction was to move forward through time, so Celia envisions several months into the future. A new scene appears: She's seated in a courtroom, on trial for murder...the murder of the couple's small child, stillborn. She hears the piercing sound of the gavel come down with the pronouncement, "Guilty of sorcery," as two men drag her out of the courtroom. A blood-chilling fear courses through her. The husband and wife are seated at a wooden table that she passes. The husband rises and yells, "Take her out of my sight—to hell with her." Her sentence: death—a burning at the stake.

Nearly unable, Celia looks further into the future. The images are almost unbearable as flames are lit beneath her tied feet. Most vivid is the smell…the horrific scent of her own burning flesh. Shaking, crying, Celia tries to remember what instructions Ray outlined next. She tries deep breathing, tries to concentrate and then, she recalls…it is the most important part. Ray said, "Ask your guides what is relevant to your present life about your soul's incarnation in the past. Hear your soul's lessons." She summons her guides and stills her mind.

"You have endured grave injustices during various incarnations as a woman on Earth," she is told by her guides. "In this life, you have withstood the greatest injustice of all—the betrayal of a young girl by her father. It is intended that you transmute this darkness and victimhood, eclipsing it with light and love. This is your divine mission; if accomplished, you help empower women. As a midwife—your soul's incarnation in a previous life—you relied upon sources of great knowledge accumulated from generations of women that came before you. You were among many women, tens of thousands, condemned for your power, designated as witches, executed on legal grounds. Through the denouncement of one woman and then another, in successive generations throughout the ages, the divine feminine has struggled against annihilation. Yet, without the balance of female energies of love and compassion, the Earth will falter. Balance must be restored for survival. The planet Earth is at a critical juncture. Many men and women, like you, are now positioned to create a new Earth—a sacred place where your neighbor is as worthy as yourself, where war is replaced with peace, where scarcity is replaced with abundance, where love, not fear, reigns over the sacred planet. This worthy goal, Earth's intended outcome, requires the energetic balance of the feminine."

Next, Celia sees a circle of men and women standing before her.

Unrecognizable to her, the circle comprises her celestial parents and the Council of White Light, whose twelve members granted her Earth assignment fifty years ago. In celebration of her presence, signaling a return to her knowledge and power, they usher her into the center of their glowing ring, and in that sacred spot, Celia's memory is restored.

Lady Kamara runs toward Celia and holds her tight. "My beloved daughter, your achievements have brought you home!" she says, tears streaming down her cheeks. "I am beyond happiness to hold you in my arms." Celia feels enormous love pouring forth from Lady Karmara's heart, a love Celia has yearned for her whole life.

Lord Myran approaches and encircles both women within his flowing gold robe. Two tiny faeries trailed by tiny stars dart above the reunited threesome, giggling, then settle onto Lord Myran's shoulder, as he directs his calm, deep voice to Celia: "Our dearest daughter, the light of our lives, congratulations on your inauguration. In your new station, you will joyously behold and navigate two worlds—the world of earthly bodily inhabitance and the world of divine spirit from the highest heavens. Your presence brings us overflowing bliss, for you have been greatly missed, but the light of your love, having usurped the rule of fear, will remain on Earth to be shared with men and women there. This dawn follows the darkest night, when not a moon or planet—Mercury, Venus, Mars, Jupiter or Saturn—illuminated Earth. On this auspicious day, your day of commencement, a harmonic convergence with the Great Central Sun of the Pleiades takes place." He smiles and lifts his gaze upward, then raises his arms up high, his golden robe glittering.

Lady Kamara, smiling with pride for her daughter's achievements, raises her right hand, palm up, from which an iridescent violet light shoots a thousand feet high, then cascades down—a towering fountain of light encompassing the group.

"A tone shall sound out," she heralds, "for this planetary alignment, a harmonious chord to harbinger the dawn of the collective dream enabled by lightworkers stationed on planet Earth including our dearest daughter, and all across the universe, who shine their love."

Wearing silver robes trimmed in opals, their glossy black hair braided into elaborate buns, the women from the Council of Light of which there are six, slowly walk toward Celia and her parents, create a circle around the reunited family and link hands. Their strong, soprano voices ring out like bells, resonating in perfect harmony, heard by women far and wide throughout the lands, interpreted as a summoning of power, a call to action.

Initially, the reverberations are barely discernible...

In Cincinnati, Ohio, Helen Whittner, seated across the dinner table from her husband Charles Whittner, Jr., who during their 20 years of marriage has never washed a dish, asks her dearest beloved if he wouldn't mind pitching in, just a bit, by cleaning up the dinner things, while she finishes her tea.

After nursing two-month-old Glenna, her fifth child, to sleep, Abigail Smith of La Grange, Wyoming, announces to her husband, Carl, "Retire to the Bible tonight because you won't get any more action until you agree to use birth control."

In Sydney, Australia, Miriam Malley raps on the office door of her petty and peevish boss, Edward Short, at Short & Sons Cleaning Supplies, and gives two weeks' notice, to follow her dream of going to law school.

In a moment of insight and clarity after Earl left their 22-year marriage for a co-worker seventeen years her junior, Carly Inez places a call to the office of Dr. Wesley Graves canceling her breast enlargement surgery.

However, within days, more sweeping changes occur...

Nina J. Butterworth, CEO of Allied Airways, announces that the company will give 10-percent of annual profits, totaling approximately $400,000, to battered women's shelters throughout London.

Betty Fran Johnston, 18, of Walpole Massachusetts, bravely comes forward, describing the rape to the county police department.

While her husband is at work, Andrea Penvere hastily packs and puts

Paige, her three-year-old daughter, and Brian, her newborn son, in the Civic and heads to safety at her sister's condo in Florida, after enduring two years of escalating physical and emotional abuse by her husband.

An undercover crackdown to expose the trafficking of teen girls in Nepal results in the arrest of four ringleaders. Nearly 90 girls are released, who help police rescue nearly 100 more.

A donation of nearly two million dollars is slated by an anonymous donor to build a hospital for pregnant women in Somalia.

. . .

Celia awakens feeling transformed. Her heart has opened wide. Her gratitude for the knowledge of her celestial heritage and her loving parents knows no bounds. She paints a watercolor portrait of Lady Kamara and Lord Myran and titles it *My Home*.

Yet, her day-to-day remains, in most ways, the same; it is simply enacted from a different place, an altered attitude of love and gratitude, and the relief of knowingness. Life rambles on, but more peacefully and with more gratitude. So, she finishes a grant application to meet a pending deadline for Coalition for Change, goes food shopping for her neighbor who has the flu, drops off a package for her at the post office. During her daily meditations, she connects with her celestial parents and these visits leave her feeling deeply loved. She is not immune to emotion and not completely free from the old tapes of her ego, but catches them turning on with the first loop around. And while less energy is expended on negative self-talk, which fuels her physical state of well-being, it is not until early March that Celia's health shows marked signs of improvement. Dr. Pierce suggests a retesting of her mercury levels—now that her detox regimen is at the six-month mark—and her levels are half of what they were. He tweaks her vitamins and minerals and she continues her protocol. She learns from her guides that certain cleanses and healings of the body must be enacted by a combination of spiritual and earthly means.

The following week, Celia researches witch hunts to validate her insights about her previous life. She was familiar with the American witch trials in Salem, Massachusetts in the late 17th Century, but had not heard of what was called "The Burning Times" throughout Central Europe. She's shocked to read that roughly 100,000 witch trials occurred between 1450 and 1750 resulting in 40,000 to 50,000 executions, mostly in Germany, France and Switzerland. Of those killed, approximately three-quarters were women, the research revealed. Many of the women accused and killed were poor, elderly or unmarried, and there was also documentation of targeting midwives, blamed for impotence, blindness, stillbirths and miscarriages. Many were killed in public, often en masse, by hanging or burning. She eagerly consults art books to access costuming and finds German paintings of women in the late 1500s dressed almost identically to her attire in her past life recollection.

...

In early April, the last winter snow of Sedona melts and beneath the bright white blanket covering the earth, seemingly against all odds, flowers begin to grow, the tiny tips of crocuses reaching for the sun. After landing two sizable grants in short succession that month from national organizations for Coalition for Change, Andy Mack calls to see if she might be interested in a public relations spot—his longstanding employee has given notice. She can work from home, he says, as long as she attends the biannual conferences in New Mexico. The job would entail obtaining media coverage to help publicize the cause and continued seeking of funds. She thinks that the salary is in the low range, but he assures her it's just a start, proposing a raise at the end of year-one. She assumed she would apply her newfound energies to her painting career or go back to teaching in the fall having missed her creative output, the exuberant energy of her students and their creative spirit. Yet, she evaluates her options based on what would be the most meaningful, how she could best serve, and accepts the job.

In preparation for her first assignment, Andy e-mails Celia a list of people who have successfully created self-sustainable lifestyles—several are in Arizona, where the plentiful days of sun encourage reliance on solar. She is instructed to interview them and hopefully nab a newspaper or magazine article about "green lifestyles," to promote ways to diminish energy consumption. She drives to the local thrift shop, Sedona Rags and Sashes, to buy something new to wear for the interviews. Most of her clothes, from her recent years teaching school, are stained with paint and too large; she has lost weight from her strict diet of vegetable juices, organic fruits and vegetables, and low-fat protein, prescribed by Dr. Pierce. There are several pretty dresses in her size. Her favorite find is an off-white velvet dress with a scoop neck that flounces down to just above her knees. It's snug and surprisingly, with her 50th birthday behind her, she can wear it gracefully.

On the first official day of her new job, she pairs it with low-heeled brown ankle boots and a new pair of off-white lace stockings—her one extravagance, which she bought at a local boutique. Her hair has started growing back and while it's still thinned, she had it styled it in a short bob to her chin with bangs. It's the haircut she wore many years back during her years in college. She wonders if she's too old for this getup, but decides she likes it, as she stands before the mirror. For the first time, her reflection beams back pretty.

She interviews a young couple who own and run an organic farm in West Sedona, supplying specialty shops with produce and baked goods. Their fruits, vegetables, honey, and breads travel no more than 500 miles to market and their farming practices are all sustainable.

Next, she drives further west—about 30 minutes—to Cottonwood, where she intends to tour the grounds of EcoHouse Designs—an architectural firm designing sustainable buildings. When she called, the receptionist said that the rest of the staff was away at a conference all week, but she could stop by the office and take a walking tour of their "green compound," then, schedule a formal appointment, if she wished, for the following week. As she heads west, she hopes that the place isn't already vacated for the weekend—it's already 2:00 on a Friday.

Rosemont Lane is easy to miss, the receptionist had said. If you hit Rural Route 4, you've gone too far, and indeed, Celia has to U-turn and then head north on Rosemont, which becomes a dirt road two miles up the mountain. It's a steady climb, and she crawls along at 10-miles-per-hour to avoid kicking up too much dust. The view toward the red rock mountains of Sedona is glorious as she drives higher and higher, until she reaches towering sunflowers, their thick stalks at least six-feet high, framing the painted yellow and green sign announcing EcoHouse Designs. As she drives through the entrance, she can see a cluster of buildings—four buildings in all—dotting the mountainous landscape. "Oh, my," she announces aloud to herself in the car, viewing the contemporary clean-lined buildings, lying low, tucked into the land as if they emerged right out of the earth. She's never seen structures hug the land like that. She's reminded of the architecture of Frank Lloyd Wright, who had a compound and school in Scottsdale called Taliesin West. She took Cosette for a public tour there years ago. As Celia drives closer, she can see solar panels atop cantilevered roofs shading decks and porches. Flowering trees and bushes of bold pinks and reds put the finishing touches on the composition. She pulls her car to a small sign that reads *Office*, cuts the ignition, grabs her pen and notebook, and ventures inside.

A sleek black desk with a high-backed, red-lacquered chair sits empty. A vase filled tight with white lilies looks pretty in a shaft of sun. "Hello," she calls out after standing there for a minute or so, waiting. "Is anybody there?" She hears footsteps and then the rear door swings opens. She can't believe her eyes. Is she dreaming? There stands Sloan Ford. She hasn't seen him in over 25 years, but he looks just like he did at School of Visual Arts—she'd recognize him anywhere. She's speechless; can't utter a word.

"Celia Barrens! I can't believe it. It's really you." His smile is ear to ear.

"What are you doing here?" she asks, incredulously.

He looks confused and then, laughs. "Now wait—that's my question," he says. "This is my home and architecture studio."

"Oh, my Lord," she says. "I had no idea. I mean, I was…I am…writing an article for Coalition for Change and your receptionist said no one would be here this week and I could come by to take a look and, well I had no idea that EcoHouse Designs was well, *you* and…" She suddenly stops. She knows she's rambling.

"I was in California. I flew back early to prep for a new client proposal."

"How did you wind up, of all places, in Arizona?" she asks.

"I came out here almost twenty years ago—did a fellowship at Taliesin West—Frank Lloyd Wright's architecture school. I've been building my business and this place since. I was probably a bit ahead of the curve and now, after some pretty lean years, the whole green thing is finally taking off. To everything there is a season," he says, and smiles. "But, tell me about you," he continues. "What's Coalition for Change? Where are you living? It's so great to see you, really. How are you?"

Sloan steps forward and puts his arms around Celia and hugs her. She thinks her knees might buckle out from under her. Oh, how she longs to linger in his arms. A sudden heat envelopes her inner thighs and shoots up like a flame. Is this desire? It's a feeling she left behind so many years ago, she forgot its power. When he lets go of his hold, he touches her bangs with the tips of his fingers, then her cheek and says, "How is it possible? You look the same."

They spend the afternoon touring his compound. As he speaks of reusable and renewable materials and reducing the impact of buildings on the environment, walking the rows of his organic garden, her thoughts drift to his straight blond hair, now layered and graying, falling over his high forehead. He's still lean and he moves like a gazelle...long, swift, graceful strides, so she can hardly keep up with him. His forearms, beneath the rolled sleeves of a crisp, royal blue button-down shirt, hanging loose over faded Levis, are as she remembered them...sinewy, now bronzed from the Arizona sun. Lingering for long stretches as the conversation veers off-track from her work assignment, she sees he's lost his shyness and seems so much more grounded, centered, in control. His bright blue eyes lock into hers when he speaks and light up when she answers him, in delight. She thinks it might just be the blaring afternoon sun, but she feels she might melt. As he shows her his sprawling sunlit studio, where he now employs four full-time architects, he's proud, but admirably humble. Photographs on the walls display recent commissions—an ultra-contemporary waterfront housing complex (waterfront structures are his area of expertise), an administrative complex at a California university, and a church in upstate New York. All the buildings are sleek and energy-efficient and several of his designs have won prestigious awards.

She learns that Sloan was married for 16 years to a woman named Trina, a model he'd met in New York. Cole, their son, lives in Hong Kong, managing a small software company. Their marriage was rocky. Trina struggled with addiction to pills. Two years ago, she left Sloan for the head carpenter at EcoHouse Designs. That relationship busted up soon after and she came running back, but Sloan said he could never trust his heart to her again. He also saw, after some distance from her, that things hadn't been right with them for a long time.

Celia releases all her secrets and they talk for hours. She tells him about her paintings, her marriage, her daughter, her return to school, and her teaching, and then, reveals her long road to recovering her health. Hesitantly, she tells him of her work with Ray and Kerrigan. He's fascinated and supportive and she feels so relieved to open herself to him. It's as if they've never missed a beat—their closeness comes back so easily, even though so much has passed unshared between them.

They swap stories about other students and teachers they know from college. "Did you hear what happened to The Wolf?" asks Sloan. Celia looks puzzled. "Oh, wow. You don't know. It was huge, tragic, really. It was even in *The New York Times*. That's where I read about it. He had an affair with a freshman student a couple years back—a prodigy of some kind. You've never seen anything like it. This kid could draw—a little Leonardo. They published one of her drawings. So, her father was a bigwig attorney in Greenwich, Connecticut. The family was loaded—steel money, if I remember. The rub was she turned out to be a minor—not yet 16 when she started college—one of those whiz kids, who gets bumped ahead in school. Well, the courts really slammed him. They got him on charges of sexual assault and child molestation and sent him to prison for 10 years. I didn't see it, but I heard from Chuck Atkinson that the whole mess was featured on one of those investigative TV shows." Celia thinks she might fall over. She feels sorry for The Wolf, but wonders if, maybe, he got his comeuppance. Sloan follows with a few more tales of students and teachers he's heard about over the years. She asks if he knows anything about Dr. Applegate, her former art history professor, and learns that she and her husband lived in Africa for a year, helping build schools.

They make their way to the kitchen, where Sloan puts on the kettle for herbal tea, while they eat strawberries from his garden seated at a round oak table. He tells her more about Trina, now ready to release more details about his marriage for which he feels sorry and ashamed. Trina had tried to win him back and he wanted no part of it. Just before the holidays, a year ago, he says, she took an overdose of sleeping pills. No one found her for days. Her parents sent the police to her house on Christmas Eve when she didn't show up for her parents' holiday dinner.

"I went through a million emotions. It's been a rough road," he says, his eyes welling with tears. "I went into therapy, then did a whole New Age thing—began meditating, seeking answers from God. That winter was pretty dark." As a tear slides down his cheek, Celia reaches to hold his hand. He lowers his eyes and softly says, "I no longer loved her. That's the truth. It was hard to bear. The guilt nearly ate me alive."

Leaning close, he rests his head on her shoulder and she strokes his arm, then gently kisses the top of his head. He smells earthy, yet clean, and his hair is still warm from the sun. She wants to run her fingers through that soft hair, take him in her arms. He lifts his chin and is kissing her; at first gently, his lips softly brushing hers, and then, with a passion she would not have expected of Sloan, he kisses her deeply, a kiss filled with longing. Celia is so surprised, so nervous, she freezes, can't feel anything and then, an animal instinct awakens that's been buried within. Slipping her hand beneath his shirt, she grabs hold of his warm, bare back and utters a soft, breathy moan, as he kisses her neck and runs his strong hands over her velvet dress, over her breasts to her waist and holds her there, tight. "Celia," he whispers, "I've always loved you. How did you find me?" He lifts her by the waist to stand and leans her against the wall, pressing himself fully against her. The tea kettle sounds a high-pitched whistle and they both laugh. "Pretty steamy," says Celia, smiling, as he releases her and turns off the burner.

Celia's mind tumbles with conflicting thoughts. She needs time to think, to think this through. "Sloan," she says, as her returns to embrace her. "It's not that I don't want you. Oh, Lord, I do. I just feel, well, scared. It's so fast. I need to catch my breath."

He cradles her face in his warm palms and gently kisses her forehead. "I know. I know. I want you to feel safe. You can. You can feel safe with me. I promise you." She lets his words enter her heart. They're real. She knows it through and through with the realization that having manifested real love in her own heart, she has now attracted it from another. "Will you stay?" he asks, taking hold of her hand and leading her to bed. He enters her slowly, moaning, whispering her name over and over. With each thrust, his eyes seek her permission and simultaneously beseech her that he cannot stop, until they reach the heights of pleasure in unison. It is an ecstasy she has never known.

They sleep tangled in each other's arms, then wake to make love again just before dawn. Mid-morning, Celia opens her eyes to the light streaming through the large picture window and turns to look at Sloan, still asleep, his blond hair circling him on the pillow like a golden sun. She unwraps his arm from her waist and sits up to get out of bed. He stirs and reaches for her, pulls her back and whispers, "Don't go. Don't ever go." She kisses his palm and places it beside him.

"I'll be right back." He smiles, pulls up the covers and closes his eyes.

Celia puts on Sloan's shirt and heads into the kitchen. She pours a glass of orange juice and takes out the large bowl of glistening strawberries and holding the thick green stems, eats two sweet-as-sugar berries seated at the kitchen table. She wanders outside to a slate patio off the kitchen, where several terracotta pots encase thickly planted herbs, crouching to lower her face, inhaling rich basil and sweet mint and then, follows a narrow path that curves around the east side of the house, where a pale blue canvas awning shades a wood deck—maybe four-feet square. She has to duck under the awning to step into this hidden space, where she finds a cushion placed before a wooden table, decorated with varied objects. It's a little altar...it's Sloan's meditation space and she wonders if she's prying, but she can't resist, kneeling to look at all the things he's put there...a photograph of Frank Lloyd Wright's most famous house, called Falling Water; a large, thickly ridged conch shell containing the burnt ends and ashes of incense and the wax bottom of a candle. There's a framed yellowed photograph of his son Cole, he's about six or seven, seated on a sailboat, his hair windblown, smiling. He has Sloan's long, lean physique and sandy coloring. A small book, a field guide to birds, is open to a page showing a Purple Martin—she wonders about the significance of that. And then, astonished, she sees it. She gasps, reaching out to take hold of a small silver-framed photograph of Paramahansa Yogananda.

A sudden wind shakes the flap of the canvas overhead and startled, Celia quickly returns the photo to the table and steps back outside. As she rounds the corner she sees two cats—one is black with white mitts, the other is white with black mitts. Aware of her approach, they head for the door and meow. She recalls having seen two cat bowls in the kitchen, so she lets them scurry in, but watches them scamper straight for the bedroom, ahead of her. When she reaches the bedroom, she sees they've jumped onto the bed and seemingly have taken their assured spots, curling up with Sloan. Half-asleep, he reaches for their heads and rubs their foreheads and ears, murmuring some endearment that Celia can't make out. Celia slips out of Sloan's shirt and crawls in with the crew.

ABOUT THE AUTHOR

Amy Abrams, former publishing executive at art magazines including *Art & Antiques*, is fiction editor of a literary magazine and author of an illustrated book about Pop artist Bill Schenck. Her stories about art, culture and travel are found at *The Wall Street Journal*, *Art in America* and Village Voice Media.

The Cage and The Key is her debut novel.

To learn more about *The Cage and The Key* and Amy Abrams, visit:
TheCageandTheKey.com

Amy loves to hear from readers. Contact her at:
Amy@TheCageandTheKey.com

www.ingramcontent.com/pod-product-compliance
Lightning Source LLC
Chambersburg PA
CBHW020416180626
46812CB00003B/1006